Deceit

By

Carol Lynn Patterson

Deceit
ISBN: 9798810677024

Book design by Reginald Dupree, Final Draft Design
Book layout by Donna Owusu-Ansah, Inspiring Creativity Ministries

Carol Lynn Patterson
www.setcaptivesfree.com

Acknowledgments

Sincere thanks to Shaun Saunders for helping me birth this book, those survivors who shared their stories with me, and the sisters in my crew who encouraged me throughout the creative process in ways big and small.

Doris,

Abundant blessings of discernment upon you!

Carol

This book is dedicated to those:

- Who have rushed into marriage because church and/or society has made them feel incomplete as singles;

- Who are in, or have been in, abusive relationships – emotionally, physically or psychologically;

- Who know people in abusive relationships; and

- Resilient ones who have overcome the heartache of deception.

Memory

In remembrance of my wise mother, Sadie, and my protective father, Douglas.

Chapter 1

Accomplished Here, Alone There

Not sure why I woke up dreaming about L.C. laughing and saying, "There's not a phony bone in your body." He's right. The truth is always better than lies and deceit. Mommy always told me – ever since I was a kid, "What goes around comes around. And you reap what you sow." I couldn't agree with her more. That's why I'm a truth-teller who deals with people above board. Might as well be. Eventually, the truth always comes out, whether you're ready for it or not; and when it does, everything in the house that's sleeping must wake up.

Speaking of truth, I honestly have no idea what I want to do for my birthday this weekend. I don't even know what I want to wear to tonight's *Who's Who*, invitation-only, red carpet, work party. (Wish I could bring my friends there.) *Hmm.* The day is so full that I can't get to my favorite boutique. I guess I'll shop in my closet and wear that black sleeveless Gucci V-neck dress.

Simple and sexy. That'll work and so will an early departure.

"Hello. Yes, this is Brooke. Thank you for your early morning birthday wishes. Yes, it's going to be a party. Yes, I'll save a dance for you. Ok! See you there! Ok! Alright then, Bye—tell him I'll see him in the office. Yeah. No...no problem! OK! Ok Bye!"

Man, it takes forever to get off the phone with these pretentious co-workers. This little boy know he don't like me. He has a phony skeleton! Mike Jr.'s been at the firm for two months, and already he's The Golden Child. Literally he's a child –25 max – fresh out of law school. The only reason he's attending tonight is because his father is one of our major clients. But Mike and I have to play nice. *Ok, Lil Mikey, let's have one dance at the Who's Who party so you can cleanse yourself of white guilt.* He's sweet, though. In a few years, he'll be ready to take on the world.

Ring. Ring.

"Hey...Thanks! It's been an amazing 33 years...I'm getting ready for work and the meeting is today...Please stop asking me that, girl. You know I'm happy with whatever you give me OK. Talk to you later."

I don't know how many times I can stand to hear the rhetorical question, "So, what do you give a woman

2

who already has everything?" Especially on the day of my birthday. The answer is simple: something else. Who doesn't need another spa day? Who'd turn down a bonus Convertible for the summer months? No wise woman would. Coco Channel says it best, "The best things in life are free. The second best are very expensive."

Life is really looking up for me! God has really been good. 33 years old today. Life, health, and strength – free. Graduate of Duke Law School – very expensive. Doing what I love at a law firm I love. There's nothing to complain about. *Brooke Rivers is killing the game.*

I never thought I would be where I am right now. Growing up in the suburbs of North Carolina gave me the best of both worlds. Humility and hospitality were in the air I breathed. I was taught to respect my elders and to say no to anything that was beneath God's best for me. I took every lesson I learned from Mommy and Daddy to heart and applied them to my life on purpose.

I didn't expect to accomplish so much so quickly. I didn't expect to graduate summa cum laude of my undergraduate class, and I certainly didn't expect to pass the bar the first time I took it. I can honestly say I am truly blessed. I earn a great salary. I've worked with some phenomenal A-list clients, and my parents are healthy and still in love. If God doesn't do another thing,

I'm really content with what He's already done. However, like any other goal-oriented, career-minded professional would, I have my eye on the prize and pressing toward the mark of the high call of partner. I'm a focused woman with a plan. Partner. It's a double entendre. My *professional* goal is to become the first Black female partner of the largest entertainment firm in all of Greenwich, Connecticut – L. C. Westbrook & Associates. And my second, more *personal* goal, is to meet the partner of my dreams. I never thought my goal to make *law* partner would be attained before my goal to be the right man's *life* partner. Never imagined I'd end up sacrificing one for the other. But the longer I live, the harder it seems to be to become successful professionally and to nurture a fulfilling personal relationship with a tall, dark-skinned, fine man who loves the Lord, and doesn't bite his nails. Of course, his salary should be relatively commensurate to mine. Since we didn't meet in law school, he doesn't have to have the career or clientele I do, but he does need passion, confidence, and swag. I can't be tiptoeing around his insecurities and accommodating his internal dysfunctions. I refuse to apologize for being one of the best entertainment lawyers in the nation. To quote Olivia Pope, "If you want me, earn me!"

Every quality, self-respecting woman needs to not just know her worth, but own her worth. Ownership is attractive. Confidence is sexy. Not sure why it took me 30 plus years to see it. But now that I've figured it out, I'm communicating my value to the world, and I'm adding tax. Like Mommy says, "Those who are for you won't leave, and those who aren't can't stay." For too long, I discounted my desires and dreams for miniature crumbs on the table of half-capable men. That ain't happening no more. I've entertained the idea of dating someone special and allowed my career to become my boo. I snuggle up with work almost every night. Making partner will soon make it all worthwhile. Meeting the right man would be a nice little bonus on the side, Jesus.

Speaking of making partner, let me respond to my boss about our meeting on Friday. L.C. Westbrook runs a tight ship. He's the boss you don't want to run into in the hallway in the morning because he'll invite you into his office for coffee and keep you there for hours shooting the breeze about golf and classical music. But he's good at what he does and very intentional about what he says and what he doesn't say over email. Whenever L.C. sends these ambiguous, "I would like to meet with you" emails without a subject line, you know a prime case, a bonus, or a promotion is forthcoming. He's a code I cracked a long time ago. And I'm the only one in the firm with the track record and experience to match the position. Can't come across too cocky. Humble is the way. I'll reply with a quick note acknowledging receipt of his email, and then I'll wait for the offer I've been praying for. My personal 33rd New Year is already starting off strong! I just hope he doesn't try to play me with the pay. I have no problem asking for what I want, and proving that I deserve it.

Ooh! It's 7:00 a.m., I gotta get going!

Chapter 2

Family Matters

The whole ride is a blur. All I really remember is some of the music that washed over me as I made the journey back to that familiar patch of land down in North Carolina. My mind was in 1,000 different places at once so I can't remember any of the scenery, any of the twists and turns, just India Arie and Chrisette Michele.

By the time I arrived at the house, Mommy was milling around making some lunch and taking out the old photo albums and Daddy was camped out on the porch with a cold drink waiting on me. Before I could get all the way into the driveway, I could hear Mommy from inside the house, "Hey baby!"

Daddy smiled with his eyes, like he always does, and got up to help me with my things while Mommy emerged from the house with a pitcher of orange lemonade and two more glasses – one for me and one for her.

It had been a little while since I had been home. No other place felt and smelled like this. It melted my heart, just like I was a girl again, to be fussed over. Then came the hugs. My parents give the kind of hugs that make the world stand still for a few moments. And somehow today they were even better, even tighter. When Daddy hugged me, it was almost like he didn't want to let me go, like he was storing up this moment, breathing it in…to last forever.

When I finally got my things into the house and surveyed everything, Mommy rushed us all back out to the porch. "It's been too long. Too long. How was your trip?"

"It was good, Mommy! Got here before I knew it," I responded.

"How did the car do?" Daddy asked with one eyebrow raised with concern. "Everything alright? Need me to look at it while you're here, make sure you're good for the ride home." I couldn't help but smile. Daddy's still fixing cars to show his love and Mommy's still fixing food to show hers.

"Daddy, it's a nearly brand new $40,000 car. It's fine. No need to get out there in this heat," I chided playfully.

"Yes," Mommy agreed. "Hot as it is, nobody needs to be anywhere near a hot engine. Plus, she just got here, Daniel, and you've got her back on the road headed up North already!"

"That's right, Mommy. All I'm thinking about right now is you two and this orange lemonade," I said as I sipped the cold elixir. Mommy made the best orange lemonade in the world. On hot days she would make delicious lemonade, the same way her mother made it years before, and she would add orange concentrate into it. To this day I've never tasted anything quite like it anywhere else. There is something so delicious about the mixture of sweet and just a little bit of sour.

"So, what have y'all been doing lately?" I asked Mommy as I watched her fidget with a spot of something on her blouse. The usual answer came back: "Much of nothing."

Daddy nodded his agreement while shaking his glass just a little to let his ice cubes sink deeper into his beverage.

"So how are y'all doing then? How you feeling?" I asked them as I settled deeper into the comfy chair Mommy had set out for me on the porch beside theirs.

"We're good, baby. Blessed and feeling good," Mommy said.

"How 'bout you, Daddy?" I asked, noticing that Daddy looked a little conflicted when I asked how they were. "Your Daddy's good, too," Mommy shot before he could speak. She said it a little bit too fast though, and Daddy didn't look much like he wanted to continue the current line of conversation.

"Uhn hunh. All is well, baby. How's work and everything? We want to hear about *you,* Brooke."

"Things are great at work" I replied. "I think I'm about to get some great news from my boss about a promotion soon. And I can't wait to fly y'all up to celebrate. Daddy, I got something special for you planned already. As a matter of fact, I'm gonna go ahead and book the tickets while I'm here so you two can let me know what works for you. I know it's busy at the church this time of year, Mommy, so we can think through…"

Before I could finish my sentence, Daddy looked at me with sorrow behind his eyes and said quietly, "Baby, I can't fly anywhere."

This made no sense. My Daddy had never minded flying before. "Why not, Daddy?" I asked. "Don't tell me you're afraid of flying all of a sudden. Remember you flew up North to see me when I…"

He cut me off again, this time his voice sounded weak and shaky, like he might cry. "No, baby. I'm not afraid, I just *can't* fly."

"Daniel, let's enjoy this moment a little bit. She just got home. Can't we talk about this later?" Mommy fussed nervously.

Now I knew something was wrong and could barely keep my composure. "Talk about what later, Mommy? What are we talking about, Daddy? Why can't you fly?"

"My doctor doesn't want me flying right now because of the recycled air and all that. We were thinking about surprising you and flying up there a little bit ago, but he said it's not good for me… because of how intense the chemo is."

I couldn't breathe.

I couldn't breathe or think or even move. Before I knew it, I had dropped my glass and tears were streaming down my face.

"*Chemo?* Daddy, why didn't you tell me?"

"We didn't want you to worry about us," Mommy whispered through tears. "Everything is gonna be alright. We're still believing God."

By the end of the conversation, I found out that Daddy had been diagnosed with advanced stage cancer months before and that the doctors were all but sure it was unbeatable after trying intense chemo with no results.

In just a few minutes, my life, which felt so perfect in almost every way on the drive down, had been turned completely inside out. I didn't know what to think, what to say, what to do. Something indescribable happens when the man who had always been your protector and your strength tells you that his body is weak, riddled with cancer, and shutting down.

The rest of the conversation is as much of a blur as the car ride there. But one small part stands out, perfectly etched into my memory, and it haunted me for years. After too many tears and sobs to count – between Mommy and I mostly – I remember Daddy telling me, "Baby, don't let this shake you. Keep living your life. We didn't say anything because we didn't want you to shut down and waste these precious months on fear and worry. Brooke, if you want to do something for me, keep living. Enjoy your career. Have fun. Find somebody and enjoy the kind of love your mother and I have." Here his voice began to crack like I had never heard and it destroyed me to hear such weakness and vulnerability in my Superman.

"That's the only prayer I have for you that's still unanswered. I pray that you experience...That you'll get married and have children." He got misty eyed as he finished the rest. "I always thought I would live to see my grandchildren. I always wanted…"

"Come on, stop this now, Daniel," Mommy pleaded. "Let's go on inside so you can lie down." Daddy limply nodded his agreement and slowly stood up to walk back to their bedroom. "I'm tired, baby," he said as he walked into the front door. Mommy got up and held on to him, walking with him to the back. In the warm North Carolina afternoon, I sat on the porch alone for what felt like an eternity, grappling with the horrific reality they had just revealed to me.

Welcome home, Brooke.

Chapter 3

Some Kinda Set-up?

I didn't even have the mental strength to drive back home at the end of the trip. Spending the week living through all the fresh pain of hearing about Daddy's cancer coming back had drained me beyond belief.

On the way down there, I was excited about the prospect of home-cooked meals, playing Gin Rummy, laughing at old stories, and watching the days slip away out on that old, screened-in porch. But the trip ended up being full of doctor's appointments, tears, and introspection.

"Why didn't they tell me as soon as the cancer came back?"

"Why *my* Daddy?"

"Why hadn't I come home sooner?"

Maybe I would have noticed something and we could have made different choices about his treatment.

All I had were questions and anger as I tried to smile for them while raging inside. Halfway through the week, despite my questions and confusion, one thing was crystal clear. I wasn't going to be able to drive all the way back home like this. The day before I was to hit the road, I decided to book a flight instead and just have my car shipped back. Thinking back now, I can almost slap myself for spending all that money, but at the time money was the last thing on my mind. I couldn't shake the pain, the fear, and the sense of anger. I just wanted to get back home and back to some sense of normalcy – some things I could control.

The final day of my trip came fairly quickly. That last morning, we had a bittersweet breakfast together. Everyone tried to keep a happy face and at least get through my sendoff meal with smiles. Every time I looked at Daddy that last day though, I kept hearing his words that first day about grandkids. All week I had tried to forget it, but I couldn't shake the sense of defeat. Here I had poured everything I had into my career and trying to make partner. I had resigned myself early to the fact that I was probably going to be alone for the first few years of my career at least, to focus on my goals. I *"leaned in,"* like the books say. I broke dates to attend firm mixers. I alienated friends, canceling last minute girls' trip plans to spend weekends working on depos and drafting briefs. I gave everything, thinking I was making myself happy and making my parents proud. But the truth is, on some level, I had made a toxic trade and time was running out.

As much as I love my parents, I have never been so relieved to return to Greenwich. Riding off in the taxi to the airport I had the worst pressure headache. The pungent smell of cigarette smoke and the cheap cologne the driver was using to try to cover it up almost took me out. By the time we got to the airport, I only wanted two things: to sink into a plush first-class seat and to drift away from it all while listening to my favorite relaxation playlist. I even sprung for the $19 sleep mask I saw while grabbing a water from a little kiosk on the concourse just before boarding. I had every intention of shutting the whole world out up above the clouds.

And then I met her.

About five minutes into the flight, I noticed the slender Black woman sitting across the aisle from me who seemed like she was itching to talk. Don't get me wrong, I love seeing another Black woman in first-class, and usually I'm all for chatting a little. But not today. Today all I wanted was to block out everything and let the sounds of *"This Too Shall Pass"* take over.

But she wasn't having it. Before I could get the sleep mask on, I made the mistake of making eye contact and that was all she needed. She motioned for me to remove my headphones. *Bold!*

I reluctantly obliged, and she quickly and excitedly started. "Skee-wee," she called out, pointing to the AKA lapel pin I forgot I had pinned to my jacket. She was trying to keep her voice down enough not to disturb everyone on board with her call, but clearly, she was excited to spot a Soror.

"Shoot, she's a Soror," I thought to myself. "Now I *know* I can't ignore her."

"Hey, Soror," I mustered up, hoping to just exchange pleasantries quickly and then be free to soak up the sounds and get some much-needed sleep. But she wasn't having it.

"Hi. My name is Anita. What's yours?"

"Nice to meet you, Anita. I'm Brooke."

"Good to meet you too, Sis. Are you heading home or away? For business or pleasure?'

"I'm heading home. Back to work."

"What do you do?"

"I'm an entertainment attorney. How about you?"

"I see you, Soror. I'm a therapist. I am actually a clinical specialist; I do a lot of work with women of color around grief."

"Really?" I was actually starting not to hate that she had spoken to me.

"Yes." she replied. "I do a lot of work with highly successful women who are working through the personal losses they experience while climbing the ladder of success. Many of my clients come to me for help processing grief around disillusionment, discrimination, isolation… So many sisters struggle with loving the life they're living."

I don't know if she could see it on my face or not, but I was almost in shock. The more she talked, the more I thought to myself, "Does she know me or something? Is this some kind of set-up?"

I tried to keep my poker face on but also to signal interest. "That sounds amazing."

I had thought once or twice about the possibility of counseling for some hard moments, but never really considered it very seriously. I mean, strong Black women don't really do that, I had always told myself.

"How many of your clients are Black?"

"You'd be surprised" she replied. "I know the stigma we often attach to therapy, but most of my clients are strong, successful, independent Black women. They just want or need a little help processing all that they are and do. As you know, this world is not always the safest place for strong Black women. We're often misunderstood. Sometimes having someone to talk to is that last piece of the puzzle for women like us."

I could barely keep myself together. Somehow what this woman was saying was getting to me big time. I guess she could see it on my face because she then gave me a kind smile and reached into a small case she had beside her and pulled out her card.

"When you get home, think a little bit about what I said and give me a call. If you ever need someone to talk to, I can help you find someone in your city who is good and discreet."

"Thank you," I managed to say sheepishly. "I'm gonna take you up on that, Soror."

"I hope you do." She said as she gave me a kind smile and then returned her attention to the book she had been preparing to read.

Chapter 4

A Time to Date

I've replayed that conversation in my head every hour of every day this week. Anita truly made an impression on me and, if I'm honest, she laid bare something I have been hiding from myself. I've known (deep down) for a while that I need to talk to someone. Sometimes it's hard to pinpoint what, but there is something that has been quietly and gently nagging and nudging me just beneath the surface. Those little unnoticed nudges had gone full-on gut punch over the past few days. Dealing with Daddy's cancer returning isn't going to be easy at all and it just makes sense to find someone to process with. But knowing that I need to and finding the courage to do it are two different things.

I keep obsessing about what Daddy said about grandchildren, too. Hearing him say that his biggest regret centers around my choices did something to me. Here I've spent all of this time building and making sacrifices, excelling in undergrad, in law school, and now at the firm. And I thought everything was fine. I really felt good and full. Besides the usual momentary rumination about my choices from time to time when a relationship fell apart or when something about this law life made me angry, I had lived my life completely convinced that I was on the right path. I was genuinely happy with my career and felt fine with my choices to prioritize work over a social life. Especially since it was just supposed to be temporary anyway. I kept telling myself I had plenty of time to fall in love, get married and have children once I made partner. But Daddy's words are making me re-think everything. His cancer returning slapped me with the realization that I don't have plenty of time. My parents won't be around forever. They might not see their grandchildren. Relationship opportunities aren't guaranteed to keep coming back around. I'm afraid I've put off the wrong thing. What if I'm unable to give the man who gave me everything the one thing he wants from me?

For the first couple of days back, I maintained my sanity by throwing myself into my cases. I probably racked up more billable hours this week than I did in the whole three weeks prior. At least that might be a silver lining down the line; it certainly can't hurt when it's time for the big meeting. It's Wednesday and I'm starting to feel my flow again, especially after a few great client calls and a huge settlement offer on a case I've been working for months coming in this afternoon. I'm finally back and feeling like I can breathe.

As a matter of fact, I might celebrate and thank God for some normalcy tonight by heading to prayer service and might even stay for Women's Ministry afterward for the first time in weeks.

~~~

"Who's that?" I wonder aloud as I walk into prayer service and notice an unfamiliar brother sitting over by the organ. I feel like I've seen him somewhere before, but not sure where. He's definitely not a member here, but I guess it's possible that I've seen him visiting in times past. I never really noticed him much before, but he's catching my eye just a little tonight. Even more, he's *definitely* noticing me.

As I slip into my pew, about three away from him, I can't help but notice how engaged he is throughout prayer. You don't usually see a lot of guys my age in prayer service, definitely not unattached ones who come on their own, so it's really noticeable. He seems fully engaged and seems to know all the words to the short praise and worship songs the praise team leads before intercession starts. "Interesting," I think to myself before zeroing back in on prayer and filing this intrigued feeling away for later. I came to thank God for my business blessings and pray for my father's healing.

"Good evening, Mother," I say to one of the Women's Ministry leaders in the vestibule after prayer service ends. She's heading downstairs to the room for Women's Ministry and makes awkward small talk, clearly wondering if I'm going to follow her down to the meeting or slip off like I often do on Wednesday nights after prayer.

"I hope things are well, Sister Brooke. Been praying for you."

"Yes ma'am. Things are well," I reply.

"Good to hear. God is able!" she says as she begins to descend the first stair on her way down to open and prepare the room. "Haven't seen you in Women's Ministry in a little while," she says rhythmically, emphasizing the little while part in a way that makes it clear she think it's been more than a *little* while.

"We miss you" she says curtly over her shoulder, a little more emboldened to say her piece now since she's heading away and doesn't have to say it to my face.

"Yes, ma'am, I'm coming down soon." I reply earnestly. I really do enjoy Women's Ministry and especially Mother Bell, you just have to be in the mood for it. The mothers who lead it are not always the most... progressive or open-minded folks in the world.

"Good, very good," she says, the smile somehow audible in her words. "Looking forward to it, baby. Looking forward," she says as she disappears down the basement hallway.

I had a few minutes before the meeting was to start, so I made the rounds to hug and speak to a few folks still milling around the sanctuary.

"Hey, how are you?" the stranger from earlier said as he offered me his hand. "I was hoping I would get a chance to introduce myself tonight. I'm Ryan. Ryan Black."

Okay, I see you. In prayer meeting. Knows all the words to the songs. Not afraid to say hello and make it clear that he's interested. Not bad at all.

"Nice to meet you, Ryan. Welcome to First Baptist. My name is Brooke."

"I know. I asked my friend who invited me to church what your name was... after you caught my eye."

"Did you?" I asked coyly.

"Yes, I did," he replied. "And I was hoping I would get a chance to introduce myself and to ask for your card so that maybe we can get together soon, if you're not too busy?" he slowed down his speech and grinned through the last few words as if to dare me to feign busy-ness and miss the opportunity to experience him. He really was something else.

As we exchanged cards and flirted a little more, I felt myself feeling a level of confidence and even joy that I hadn't really felt since getting the news from Daddy. Even if I didn't move forward at all with him, it's always good to feel seen and wanted. Doesn't hurt that he loves God either! On the way downstairs to the meeting room, I felt myself smiling bigger than I had for little while. Good thing I decided to come out to church tonight.

It only took a few minutes of the meeting for me to start regretting that I stayed. Don't get me wrong. I *love* First Baptist. The people are warm and genuine, the Word and worship are on point. Usually, I enjoy the Women's Ministry meetings too, at least a little. But tonight, the mothers were on one.

"Every woman wants to get married" seemed to be the theme of the night. Somehow, even though it wasn't the chosen topic of the meeting at all, they kept managing to bring everything back to marriage. As a matter of fact, some of the older women seem to find a way to bring everything back to that on *every* occasion. Marriage. Children.

To hear some of these women tell it, that's all a woman should ever think about. As much as I love my sisters, tonight was not the night for it. As if I wasn't feeling haunted by my choices before I came here, now all I hear is, "Every woman wants to get married."

I know they mean well, but why do the church mothers always have to pronounce their judgments and thoughts on everybody and everything? Whose business is it if I get married or not? Why does it matter when or if? Before I could even think that last thought, I saw Daddy in my mind. Sitting on that porch, talking about how much he wanted grandchildren. Usually, I was able to eat the fish and spit out the bones when it came to Women's Ministry, but tonight those words just kept bouncing around in my head and my heart, "Every woman wants to get married."

When I finally whispered to myself, "Maybe they're right," it happened. At that very moment, literally at that very second, I felt my phone vibrate.

When I pull it out to check the text message discreetly, looking for a reprieve from this moment of self-reflection and second guessing everything, I see a text from Ryan. His message says, "I hope this isn't too forward, but I would love to take you out for dinner Friday night. I know it's quick, but every woman wants to be wined and dined, right?" When I read the words "Every woman wants…" in his text, I almost gasped audibly. I try not to be the person who says that everything is a sign, but in that moment, I couldn't help but imagine that maybe this was God.

~~~

"Am I actually nervous? What's going on with me? I guess it's been a little while since I've been on an actual date. Is this even a good decision?"

My mind races all the way to the restaurant. Maybe I shouldn't have accepted the date for the first night he offered. I hope I didn't come off as too available. As I'm thinking all of this, I can't help but notice how much this is grating on me. I've never been this woman. Unsure and timid and pressed about a man is not who I am. But remembering what Daddy said and thinking about the women in Women's Ministry has me tied up in knots.

I thought I would feel less anxious after therapy. Pondering what Anita said on the plane, made me decide to give her a call and ask for a good referral for someone to process with in Greenwich. She linked me with a Black woman right around my age and I got a chance to sit down with her yesterday. She didn't say too much, I guess that's how it's supposed to be. But I was struck when she mentioned that maybe I need to "color outside the lines" a little bit more and try something new and different. So here I am, about to walk into this restaurant with a man I don't know at all who I met two days ago. If this isn't something different, I don't know what is.

As I walk into the door and approach the hostess, I spot him immediately over in the far-right corner. There's something about him. He seems so present and confident. Not full of himself, but solid. As soon as he spots me, he gives me that look that tells me everything I need to know about whether I picked the right outfit. Like the perfect gentleman, as I approach the table, he rises to give me a full but respectful hug and to of course compliment me and pull out my chair. He's certainly starting off well.

"Have you been to Morton's before?" he asks as I get settled into my seat.

"Yes," I reply, "I like to come out here to Westchester from time to time on the weekends when I'm not too busy, which isn't very often these days."

"Law keeps you running, huh?"

"Yes." I see he pays attention to details. He's smooth and he knows it, this might get interesting.

"A man should never go out on a date with a beautiful woman without preparing himself with at least a little info," he replied, more than a little velvet in his voice. "With all the men who ask you out regularly, I figured I should give myself a fighting chance at standing out."

It went on like that for over an hour. By the end of the date, I knew only a few things about him for sure. He lived in the Stamford area, his mom was from North Carolina just like my parents and he had serious game. He was so attentive and interested in me and what I had to say. By the end of the date, I felt like I had known him for years, and I was opening up in a way that I almost never do on first dates. Maybe it *was* God.

As we walked outside and he escorted me to my car, I started to feel a little anxious. At first, I couldn't put my finger on what it was, but eventually I realized that I was anticipating that moment of truth. Usually, I was absolutely against a kiss on the first date. My mother always taught me to make them really work for it. But tonight, I kept finding myself wondering when he was going to signal that he wanted to kiss. And I think I would have obliged. But he remained the gentleman even then. When we arrived at my car, he told me he had a wonderful evening and looked forward to the next one. Then he grabbed my right hand in his, lifted it to his lips and kissed my hand so sweetly. It was a perfect moment to end a perfect date. Well…it was near-perfect. The only slightly awkward moment was when the bill came and he put down a coupon or gift card or something under his debit card. It felt like he was trying to hide it, thinking I didn't notice. That's the part that made it awkward. I don't mind a man who is responsible with money and wants to save on a meal. Financial responsibility is actually attractive. But the fact that he seemed to be trying to hide it made me a little uneasy. But I do have a habit of overanalyzing little things. I've let them cause unnecessary issues in dating in the past. So, all is good and I won't trip this time.

Once I settled into my car and he began to walk away to his, I felt myself exhale deeply as I cranked my engine and thought wistfully about what the next date with Ryan might be like.

Chapter 5

An Uneven Exchange

These past few days have all been a whirlwind. Daddy's diagnosis still sits in the back of my mind like an un-welcomed visitor. His request for a grandchild pops up whenever I begin to let my guard down. I've been distracting myself with thoughts of dinner with Ryan. Throughout the day, I feel myself blushing as I replay the moments. A cheesy smile makes itself at home on my face. I was pleasantly surprised to see a good morning text from him. I didn't think he would have reached out so soon. But, as snatched as I was, I wouldn't blame him. Still, I'm not trying to jump the gun. There's still a lot that I don't know. For now, I'll slow down and enjoy some much-needed happiness.

There was something else that would make me even happier, and it required my absolute focus, becoming partner. While I don't want to disappoint Daddy, I'm so, *so* close. I've been working toward and waiting for this promotion for a long time, and I've earned it. I've shown myself to be hard working, reliable, and innovative. I don't say that to be braggadocios. L.C knows what I bring to the table. In this field, and for many Black women in their fields, we have to be like Olivia Pope, "twice as good" in order to have half of what some of these *other* folks have. L. C. Westbrook & Associates has been overdue in having someone like me at the decision-making table. *Westbrook, Rivers, & Associates*…it's a sound that rings so sweetly in my ears.

I know what I'm worth. I fought to get into Duke University School of Law. I had so many sleepless nights trying to maintain my GPA. My academic prowess netted me a fellowship and through that fellowship, I was able to have a paid internship here at Westbrook. Once my internship was completed, I was brought on as an associate. Networking and negotiating are a breeze. I can handle clients big and small and add to the firm's prestigious reputation. I've never been star-struck, not even when certain A-list clients come my way. I always ensure that clients and their teams feel at ease working with the firm. Research doesn't intimidate me. On those rare instances when I make mistakes, I learn from them and carry the learning forward. One of my mistakes ended up seeming like a strategy! God is good!

Interning and being hired to work at offices located on the "Gold Coast" of Greenwich, which is known as home for hedge funds and old money, was like a dream come true. The ocean view I have from my office is stunning. Whenever I need a moment to decompress from the goings on in the firm, I just watch the boats sailing in the distance. Warm, summer sunlight is trickling through my window as I peacefully and prayerfully think things over.

Whiffs of coffee float past my nostrils. *Knock, knock, knock.* I have to resist the urge to roll my eyes at the sight of Mike Jr. smugly leaning against my office doorway with a cup of coffee. Time to be cordial.

"Hello, Mike. What brings you by?"

He flashed a smirk that left me feeling uneasy. "No particular reason. Just enjoying the view."

I know dang well this fetus isn't trying to flirt with me. What does he want? I bite back a chuckle, "Which view are we talking about?"

"The one from your window," he said with a snide tone. I was annoyed by the sound he made slurping his coffee.

"You know, I'm going to be making partner soon and this would be a nice spot for me. And I'm sure you'd make a great secretary."

The absolute audacity of the Caucasity. He's so lucky his father is one of our clients. If he wasn't, I may or may not have unleashed an unholy tongue depending on if the Holy Spirit or my flesh got to me first. Leaning over my desk, I rested my chin on my interlaced fingers. "Interesting observation, Mike, given you just got here as an *intern*. Even more interesting that you chose to reduce me to a mere secretary when I'm part of the reason why your father became one of our clients."

"And I thank you for all of your hard work, Brooke. I really do. You're right, secretary was a bad choice of words. I really meant seat warmer."

"You have a lot of nerve, kid. I hate to cut your dreams of bringing me down short, but I have a meeting with L.C. in 15 minutes. So, if you'll excuse me…"

"Oh. That's fine. I don't want to keep you. You'll forgive me for being the bearer of bad news. I know you've had your heart set on becoming partner for a while. Just figured I should warn you first. So don't shoot the messenger. Okay, Sis?"

"Life and death are in the power of the tongue, Mike. I'd be careful if I were you. And by the way, I'm not your *Sis.*"

Mike quickly turned on his heel, chuckling as he took another sip of his coffee. He nearly broke his neck trying to get out of my sight. I sighed and massaged my temples. Last thing I needed before this meeting was a headache. I started to gather my things, muttering quiet prayers to myself in hopes to calm my nerves. I fixed my crown. Mommy and Daddy raised me to never lower my head for anyone except the Lord. I strode to L.C.'s office and took another deep breath before knocking on his door. A welcoming, "Come in," could be heard from the other side of the door. I turned the handle, ready to enter into my new season.

~~~

"Wait, what do you mean you're delaying my review for partner?" I looked into L.C.'s face. His expression was gentle and seasoned with years of experience.

"I know this comes as a shock, Brooke. However, there's a bit more I need to see from you."

"Sir, what more do you need to see from me? I do practically everything…"

"That's the problem. I haven't seen you delegate or take the team approach often. I have no qualms with your work ethic, Brooke. However, I am concerned that you're heading on a road to burn out. No one can do it all by themselves. If you're going to become partner, Brooke, I need you at your absolute best, and I need you mentoring others. The decision will be postponed until I'm convinced you can carry the load for the long term. Then we'll move forward."

The feeling of deflation crept over me as I stared at my bedroom ceiling replaying the scene over and over. I wanted to throw up. Everything in me wanted to scream. *"Smiling faces, Smiling Faces, Sometimes they don't tell the truth. Smiling faces, smiling faces tell lies and I got proof..."* The Temptations crooned from my Bose speakers. I didn't believe in Jinxes, but it really felt like Mike vexed my spirit with that demonic slurping sound. First Daddy, now this? What's next?

I fumbled for my phone to turn off my Spotify. Each song that played after The Temptations' track seemed to mock me. I had no energy for that. The silence seemed to make things worse. I wanted to call someone.

Yet, I didn't want to call any of the numbers saved in my phone. I didn't want to deal with Negative Nancy's telling me I work too hard, or be placated with advice that I wasn't asking for. Maybe I should call Anita? I forced myself out of bed to go downstairs to my home office. I had put her card in my desk drawer.

"Hello, this is Dr. Anita Davis. How may I help you?"

"Hey Soror, it's Brooke. How are you?"

"Hey, girl hey, I'm good. You sound a little down. Is something wrong?"

"Do you happen to have an opening for some time early next week?"

"Hold on, let me check here…one sec…. Hmmmm…okay, perfect. I have an opening for Monday morning at 9 AM. Since you're out of the area, I can do a tele-visit with you. Does that work?"

"I can clear my schedule and travel in. Maybe getting away for the day will be good for me. 9 AM is fine." Burnout, huh? Maybe L.C. sees something I don't.

Chapter 6

Getting to Know You

Is this really a counseling office? Anita's office looked as if it could have been my best friend's living room…minus the mimosas. The space felt like a calming safe haven. Misty blue walls were accented by sleek, cream furniture. Hibiscus and Jasmine flowers called the garden style windows home. In between the usual inspirational art pieces were canvases of game-changing Black women. Ida B. Wells, Shirley Chisholm, Michelle Obama, Eartha Kitt, and Aretha Franklin to name a few. I stopped in front of Maya Angelou. It was Maya taken by G. Paul Bishop, Jr. in 1954. The *phenomenal woman* elegantly posed in a floor-length, white dress. Her hands and feet pointed and prepared to dance. Eyes shut and mouth open in breathy song. As if the snapshot wasn't breathtaking enough, the caption on the card below it left me gasping.

"You may not control all the events that happen to you, but you can decide not to be reduced by them." – Maya Angelou

I became hyperaware of the pit of anxiety that slowly formed in my stomach. Daddy's illness and his wishes, L.C.'s critiques and not making partner. All of these things were outside of my control and towering over me like skyscrapers on the brink of collapse. I can decide, huh? I take a seat in the chair closest to the window. The soft creak of a door opening and a "Hey, Soror," caught my ear. Anita daintily slipped into the room. The kimono maxi dress she wore made her appear as if she was floating. Her long dreads styled into a crowning bun and a flower tucked on her left ear. Rather than taking the seat behind her desk, she chose to sit in the one across from me.

I was a bit nervous opening up to her, given the only time I spoke to her was on the plane. Sensing my nervousness, she took the time to explain the options I had for the direction of these sessions. It was a relief. To be honest, I kind of expected the stereotypical venting session with me laying on the couch and Anita half listening. Instead, I was given the choice to talk about my feelings over a cup of tea.

Anita filled my cup with hot water from her Keurig and brought me an assortment of teas to choose from. I grabbed a Lemon Zinger while Anita went back to the machine for coffee. The session lasted about an hour. It felt good to get rid of mostly everything that was weighing on my mind. There was still a bit that I wasn't ready to share yet. I decided to schedule another session in a few weeks.

As I was leaving Anita's office to head back to my hotel, my phone vibrated a few times in my pocket. That cheesy grin resurfaced again.

> *Hello Brooke, I hope you're having a wonderful day. You have been on my mind all day. I'm sorry if I'm coming on too strong, but I would love to see you again. If you're free this weekend, one of my favorite bands is performing at a jazz club I'd like to take you to. It would be a pleasure to drink in good music while in your company. Please let me know. Ryan.*

My mind raced trying to figure out how I was going to answer. Suddenly, I heard the sound of someone's throat clearing. I look up to see that Anita was beside me.

"Everything okay, Brooke? You've been standing in the same spot for the last five minutes."

"OH! Yeah! I'm fine. Totally fine! I just…saw something that brightened my day." I sheepishly answered.

"Oh, made your day?" I could tell by her tone she wanted to be nosy. "Was it something from the gentleman that you recently started talking to?" The way she asked, she already read me dead to rights.

"You can say that. He invited me to a show this weekend but I'm not sure if I should go."

She leaned back on her heel, "Why not? You deserve to have a good time. You can enjoy the atmosphere and leave it at that if you're not feeling him."

"I know, Anita. It's just- I don't know how to explain it. There's something about him. I don't want to say I'm in love or anything drastic like that. He just knows how to make me feel. Like he could read my mind from wherever he is. I don't know…"

"Listen Brooke, we talked about this in your session. You have a lot on your plate. But don't deny yourself things that make you happy. You have to find the balance otherwise you'll suffer a blow that will be hard to bounce back from. You don't need the permission of your circumstances to live your life. Just live. That doesn't mean be silly or reckless, but you have to live." Anita may as well have been Maya Angelou at that point. I silently nodded and gave her a knowing smile.

I decided to leave Ryan in suspense and texted him after I returned home the next day.

Hello Ryan, I was pleasantly surprised by your message the other day. Sorry it took me a bit to get back to you. Yesterday, was a busy day. A jazz club sounds like it would be fun. What day and time is the show?

A beat barely passed before I felt my phone vibrate, "*The concert begins at 9:30 PM on Saturday. Would 8 PM be a good time for me to pick you up?*"

I bit my lip at the response, "*It's perfect.*"

Spotify set the mood for my Saturday night. *But if you feel like I feel, please let me know that it's real. You're just too good to be true, Can't take my eyes off of you,* Lauryn Hill sweetly sang through my speakers. *I love you baby…* I sang out as I danced around my room, gently swinging my hips in time with every word. I paused when I caught my reflection in the mirror. The glam was on goddess and my melanin popped severely.

My wine, V-neck dress had a ruffled, sweeping train, perfectly matched with my red Louboutin stilettos. Just as Jill Scott's "Golden" began to play, that familiar ping rang out.

> *Hello Brooke, just letting you know I'm 15 minutes away. See you soon.*

I did one final check in the mirror before shutting everything down. Color outside the lines and live. Okay. I got it. I got this…yeah. I couldn't understand why I felt so nervous. The last date went well. This one will too. And if it doesn't go well tonight, then it's all good. I took a deep breath and went to wait by the door. Silence hung with bated breath before I could hear the sound of a car pulling up. I waited a moment before opening the door and there he was waiting to open the passenger door. My voice caught in my throat. His dark eyes smoldered in the moonlight. What caught my attention though was our unexpected coordination. He wore a grey suit, with a burgundy dress shirt. *Lord, is this a sign?*

He spoke first, slowly making strides toward me, "Good evening, mademoiselle."

"Well, good evening to you too, monsieur. Who knew you spoke French?" I queried coyly, stifling a giggle.

"Je peux vous parler français toute la nuit si tel est votre désir, ma chère. That means, that I can speak French to you all night long if that's what you desire, my dear." He flashed a beautiful smile before taking my hand to kiss it. *Oh…My…God…Jesus who is this man and what took him so long?* "Shall we go, Brooke?" All I could do was silently nod my head.

Taking the same hand he kissed, he led me to the car. He let my hand go to open the door and help me into the car. Our destination was 45 minutes away from Greenwich and into NYC. The Smoke Jazz & Supper Club was known for bringing in big talent. I was excited to say the least.

The whole drive I could smell the soft whiffs of his cologne. I couldn't place the fragrance but I detected hints of sandalwood. It was nice, for a moment it seemed like I could get away from everything, albeit briefly.

The intimate setting of the club seemed to heighten the romantic tension between Ryan and me. The concert was amazing. I had never heard of Eric Roberson before tonight. He was more Neo-Soul than Jazz, but I didn't mind. Ryan said Roberson's "Be With You" described how he had been feeling as he daydreamed about being with me. We slow danced to a few of the songs while we waited for dinner seating to open up. Once a table opened, he again gently took me by the hand and led me to the table, stopping to pull out my chair for me. We placed our orders. I ordered the seared salmon as I was curious about how the dish would fuse chorizo, lemon, Little Neck clams and white wine parsley broth with the choice salmon. I thought that Ryan would have opted for the NY strip steak. Instead, he got the sausage & shrimp jambalaya. Now, I love soul food. Don't get me wrong. I just felt it was a little…low brow given how the evening was going. Then again, he did bring a coupon to the last date. I shrugged it off. It was only a small detail in an otherwise amazing night. By the time he brought me back home, I had already decided in my heart that I wanted to see him again.

Well, there was one other detail, but it had nothing to do with Ryan. There was a couple sitting at the table to the side of us and there was something peculiar about them. They were a nice-looking pair, had to have been in their 30s, and…on their phones the entirety of their dinner. Sis seemed to just endlessly scroll what looked to be her Instagram feed. I'm not sure what her date was looking at. One would think that if you were at dinner that you would talk face to face, smile, laugh, or something. They just seemed so disconnected from each other. Maybe they were just going through the motions of a relationship? Did they maybe want to end it, but felt they had to stick it out? Maybe they got into an argument on the way there? I don't know. Whatever their deal was, I hope Ryan and I never get to such a place where we're together yet alone.

Months passed and they were filled with more dates with Ryan. Some days we would go to the park and just talk. Other times we would go and enjoy a night on the town. I started to learn his love languages and I felt comfortable enough to teach him mine. Tender touches and kisses. Compliments post-workouts at the gym. Cooking together. My heart felt full. Eventually, I shared with him about what was going on with Daddy. I hoped in my heart that I would have enough time for Daddy to meet Ryan and maybe that he would be here long enough to give Ryan and I his blessing to start a family. Ryan said he came from a big family and what he wanted was a bit on the smaller scale. One or two children at most. That was something I was okay with. With my career, I had no intentions of being a baby machine. We settled on getting a puppy until we were ready for kids. Sebastian, a Scottish Terrier. Sebastian loved cuddling up to Ryan. His tiny body seemed to hide in Ryan's muscular frame. He was a spoiled little pup.

If Ryan wouldn't pick him up, he would whine and paw at me until I did. He also would get very jealous if Ryan and I cuddled. He would stand up on his hind legs and want to join us on the couch. Never a dull moment with a playful pooch.

Ryan saw himself as a leader. He loved connecting with people and felt a call to lead people into living their best life as God intended. He said he wasn't exactly sure if this was God calling him to ministry. I thought about it. A pastor's wife? Me? Would that mean I would be the primary breadwinner? Time would tell. He would often ask about how things were going at Westbrook. Most of the time, I would lie through my teeth. Mike Jr. was making things a bit difficult for me once he found out I didn't make partner. L.C. still felt I wasn't enough of a team player. Rumors slowly started to spread about me being difficult. I began to feel miserable. Then Ryan said something to me that I will never forget.

"Brooke, you are a smart and beautiful woman. Why are you waiting for someone like L.C. to give you a chance? You should start your own firm. With all that you've done at Westbrook, the clients would have to follow you. You have been that firm's backbone for years."

"I agree with you Ryan, but if I leave now, wouldn't that be proving him right?" The thought of leaving had triggered an underlying fear. "L.C. doesn't come across as a vindictive person. But there's not a whole lot of people who look like us in Greenwich. What if I get blackballed for trying to go? What if he tries to sabotage me if he sees me as competition?"

"Baby, look I don't think L.C. would try anything because you know that firm and all its tricks like the back of your hand. Westbrook wouldn't want to take that kind of risk. You know the law and how it can protect you. I think a firm owned by a Black woman may be a good thing for Greenwich. There may be other Brookes out there waiting for chances and opportunities. You could give them that. Baby, you can create your own lane and take over the world. You should go for it."

He reached out to stroke my cheek. Having him reassure me allowed me to take a break from being the "strong, Black woman" the world always forces us to be. "Maybe I should, Ry. Maybe I should." Would I really be able to maintain my own firm? Would it sound better as *Rivers & Associates* or *Rivers-Black & Associates*?

It would be amazing to create my own lane. I could create a fellowship so AKAs that are now in law school can have better opportunities than I had.

I couldn't believe how much Ryan believed in me. Most men get intimidated by successful women. I think I may have finally met my match.

Chapter 7

Meeting The Fitzgeralds

"At laaaaaa~ssst~ My luh~ha~ove has come alonnnng~ My lonely days are over..." The sound of my shower provided the perfect acoustics for my private joyful noise concert. The rain like stream coming from my shower head provided a complementary percussion of sorts. In my head, it was a one-night-only performance on the beaches of Hawaii. The warm, steamy air of my shower set the atmosphere for my escape to the tropical shore. My fingers gently ran through my coils, letting the deep conditioning treatment cradle every strand of hair. The smell of moringa, coconut, and hibiscus drifted in the air, a trademark of the conditioner working its softening magic. I stretched out one of the coils. I know the devil is a liar, and so is shrinkage. It was almost mid-back now. For a moment, the fantasy of my concert was interrupted by the thought of having to dry and straighten it. I dreaded the arm workout that was to come. And then I remembered, after watching a video by a well-known,

naturalista YouTuber, that I impulse bought the newest Dyson hair dryer that she reviewed. I made sure to get the bonus wide-tooth comb attachment to ensure that everything would work the way she demonstrated. It normally would have taken me over an hour and a half to dry my hair. But Jesus was on the mainline with the Dyson company because that time was cut down by an hour. I was able to go back to my mental musical number in peace. *Rinse.* Perfect timing too, I was approaching the big finish. I grabbed my detangling comb and positioned it carefully. *"And you are MY~AY~IIIIIIIINNNNEEEE~ AT LA-"*

"BABY!" a familiar voice called out, startling me in the process.

"WHAT THE- WHOA!" My life flashed before my eyes as I suddenly lost my footing in the shower. I quickly grabbed at the handlebar that I had installed in case Daddy needed it during a stay, knocking over a few of my shower gels in the process. *THUNK! THUNKA! THUNK! THUNK!*

"HOLD ON BROOKE, I'M COMING!" before I could respond that I was actually okay, a very distressed Ryan tore open my shower curtain. "BABE ARE YOU- oh…"

I watched Ryan's eyes process the situation before he looked me up and down, "OH!" Flustered, but slightly flattered, I grabbed at the shower curtain to quickly cover myself, but not before giving Ryan a few good bops with my comb. He shuffled back laughing with his hands on his head. "OUCH Brooke, that hurt!"

I huffed and closed the curtain, finished rinsing out my hair and gave it one last detangle before shutting the water off. I peeked out the shower curtain to see Ryan holding out my towel with one hand, and playfully using the other as a shield to defend himself.

"You have a nice body, Love." He sheepishly whispered.

I snatched the towel before disappearing behind the curtain, "I know, and you gotta wait for it." Wrapping the towel around me, I stuck a hand out to shoo Ryan out of the bathroom, which he kissed before scampering off. I decided to make Ryan wait for me to finish my hair before I addressed him. I could hear him playing with Sebastian downstairs. As I finished up with my hair, something struck me. *How did he get into my house?*

While Ryan and I had been together for a few months, I never gave him a key. It bothered me, but I shrugged it off thinking he may have gotten a copy made in order to feed Sebastian while I'm at work. Once done, I detoured to my room to get dressed before going downstairs. A comfy, mini tee and my favorite yoga pants.

I arrived downstairs to see Ryan and Sebastian curled up together on the couch and snoozing away. *If he's this tired with a puppy, I wonder how he'll be with kids.* I leaned over the couch to place kisses on Ryan's forehead, repeating the pattern over and over until he began to stir awake. Slightly opening one eye, he let out a soft chuckle, "Do you forgive me now?"

"Maybe," I said attempting to place another kiss on his forehead. Instead, Ryan sat up to sneak a kiss on the lips, and then another, and another. I broke off the smooch fest to make a smoothie. Ryan quickly followed suit.

"And what will make you forgive me?" he asked. He slunk behind me to sneak a few more kisses on my neck. I turned my face to nuzzle his cheek. I expected to smell the aftershave I loved on him. Instead, I smelled…

Axe. I quickly turned my head to fill my nostrils with the smell of melon instead.

"Well, surprise me." I said, trying to ignore the smell of cheap cologne that was lingering on my bae like a stalker-ish ex.

He snuck one more kiss and came around the kitchen island so he'd be able to look me in the face. "How about dinner with my family?"

I looked up at him with pleasant shock. "Your family? You mean it?"

"Of course. I think it's high time you met my mom and stepdad."

"Stepdad? Okay, and when can I meet your dad?"

"When he's not busy trying to go around the world in 80 days."

"Well, next time we should go with him. So, when did you want to do this dinner with your parents?"

"How about tonight?"

"Tonight?!"

"Well…yeah. My stepdad bought this yacht to celebrate his retirement and I thought it would be a good opportunity for them to finally meet you."

"A yacht huh? I guess you did surprise me after all. Well, I better get changed now or we'll be late. Is it a big celebration? What is the dress code?"

"Nah, it's a small get together with my stepdad, Mom and a few of their friends. I'm not changing out of my clothes so; I'd say just dress fly like you normally do. And yeah, we don't want to be late. The Hamptons aren't around the corner you know…"

I smiled and took the smoothie I began to prepare and put it in the fridge to stay cold until I was ready to make something with it. Back up the stairs I went to change into something more fitting for a yacht trip. The weather was nice and warm that day. I opted to wear a turquoise sundress and bring my floppy straw hat to keep the sun out of my face. This seemed to be record time for me to get ready. I wasn't going to miss a trip to The Hamptons for anything. Two and a half hours seemed like only minutes while in the car with Ryan. He had a knack for finding a way to fill up that space with his presence. He knew how to make me laugh and say all the right, cheesy things that made me smile. These long trips made me realize that even with all of his quirks, I really found my soulmate.

When we arrived at the harbor, I was in awe of how big the yacht in question was. It seemed a bit oversized for a small get together among friends. Ryan's mother and stepfather greeted us as soon as they saw his car pull up.

His stepfather made me think of the actor Obba Babatundé and his mother made me think of Iman. I could only imagine what his father looked like. His mother seemed to float down the deck toward us in her white, muse-like dress. Her arms outstretched, she wrapped me in them like I was her long-lost daughter.

"Bonjour, ma pêche (my peach). I'm so glad you could make it. Ryan has told us so much about you. You look gorgeous, darling." *I can see where he got the French from.* It was interesting to hear her French spoken with the honeyed twang of the South. His stepdad approached puffing a cigar, in a silk shirt, white slacks, and those ghastly, Gucci fur-lined mules. Mike Jr. had a period of time where those shoes were all he wore in the office. The thought of it sends a chill up my spine. I regain my focus from the distraction of the shoes.

"It's nice to meet you, Mrs. Black. I-"

She gestures with her hand, "Oh no, dear. That was my last name when I was married to Ryan's father."

I wanted to facepalm myself, "Oh my goodness, I'm so sorry. I-"

Ryan's mother gestured with her hand again. "No worries, ma pêche. It happens all the time. Fitzgerald is my husband's last name. So, you could call me Mrs. Fitzgerald, but I would much rather you call me, Ella."

The amount of strength it took not to laugh was almost inhumane. "A pleasure, Ella."

Mr. Fitzgerald stepped forward, puffing a few times on his cigar, before letting the cigar rest in his left hand. He extended his other hand to me for a handshake. "Nice to meet you, darlin'. The name's Francis. You can call me that or Scott." He was definitely more laid back then Ella was. But his name caught my attention too.

"Francis? Scott? I guess that must be the *key* to the two of you making beautiful music together and having such a great marriage?"

Ella perked up, "Ryan?! You weren't supposed to tell her about our music! That was supposed to be a surprise for later this evening."

Before Ryan could answer, I spoke up, "Oh no ma'am, it was only because of your names. I was just trying to make a pun."

Ella looked at me puzzled, "I'm afraid that I'm out of the loop my dear. You'll have to forgive me." She paused to look at her watch, "Oh my, we better get on board. It's almost time to go." Despite the slightly awkward intro, I was still excited to get to know Ryan's family.

The day went on full of mixing and mingling. Mr. Fitzgerald had just retired after working for Boeing for 40 years. Now that he had more free time to spend with Ella, he decided to pursue his lifelong passion for music, and the two decided to create a jazz cover band, The Fitzgeralds. They announced that they were going to perform a song before dinner. Francis began to softly play Etta James' "At Last" on the piano. (I was just singing that to myself earlier. Was this another sign?) Ella gracefully approached the mic, opened her mouth and well...bless her heart. I never would have thought in a million years I would know what a dying seagull gargling molasses would sound like but...bless her heart. When they finished, the group of 20 audience members, not including myself and Ryan, gave that awfully familiar clap. You know the one. Ella enthusiastically took a bow. Francis on the other hand, tried to hide the wince in his smile.

Dinner was exquisite. Caviar, oysters, Wagyu beef, Fois gras, white truffles. That wasn't even the full menu. My eyes almost became as big as my stomach. While we were eating, I made chit chat with Ryan's parents. Even though it had only been a few hours, they made me feel so comfortable. It was like I had known them for years. Toward the end of dessert, Ella asked a question that I found really bizarre. "Ryan, darling. I happened to bump into your friend Kelly the other day. When was the last time that you talked with her?"

Ryan looked like he wanted to melt into the table. "It's been a while, Mom."

Ella nodded as if she knew something else, "I see. Well, she looked good."

"Aight. Thanks, Mom. I'm glad to hear she's doing good. So, F. Scott, how 'bout them Giants?" Seeing how quickly Ryan tried to change the subject gave me a weird vibe. I happened to glance over at Ella in my peripheral. Maybe I saw wrong. It almost seemed like she was mocking me.

It was around 10:30 PM when we docked. We said our goodbyes and exchanged final pleasantries. Another hug from Francis and Ella. Francis gave me a tight squeeze. However, something seemed really off with Ella's hug. I tried to play it off thinking it may have been my anxiety about meeting his family getting to me. Ryan took my hand and led me to the car. For the first part of the ride home, Ryan mostly talked. My mind began swimming with thoughts. I was wondering if I should bring up this 'Kelly' person. Eventually, Ryan noticed how quiet I was. "Are you okay, Brooke?" he asked.

"Huh? Yeah, I'm just tired."

"You sure?"

"Yeah…actually…Babe…"

"Yeah?"

I looked over at Ryan, "Do you think your family liked me?" I was searching for reassurance in his face.

He flashed that smile I loved so much. "I know they loved you. They can be a handful sometimes, but they are truly genuine people."

"I'm glad. I was kind of worried a bit there. You know, Ryan, do you think in a few weeks that we can make a trip to go see my parents?"

"How about we do next weekend? I'm eager to meet your family."

"Me, too."

Chapter 8

Meeting The Rivers

Daddy had a few appointments so we had to push back our visit another two weeks. The whole drive down I was on pins and needles to see if my parents were going to like him. When we pulled up in the driveway, I could feel my anxiety coming to a head. Then Ryan's gentle stroke of my cheek eased my mind. Ryan stepped out of the car and rushed over to open my door. Mommy was just coming out to help Daddy to his favorite chair on the porch.

"Mommy! Daddy!" I called with a wave. They both looked up at us and shouted in excitement. Daddy's face had a special glow about it today. I grabbed Ryan's hand and brought him closer so they could see. "Mommy, Daddy, I want you to meet Ryan." I gestured to him, scanning their faces for any indicator of their first impressions.

Ryan had turned on his charm and introduced himself. He approached Daddy and extended his hand for a handshake. Daddy shook his hand. He paused for a moment, letting the stillness in the air permeate the moment. "You learn a lot about a man by how he shakes hands." Daddy said.

"Well sir, I hope I told you everything you need to know." Ryan's smile extended from ear to ear.

"Yes, son. You've told me all that I need to know."

Mommy interjected, "Ya'll must be tired after such a long trip. Why don't you get inside so you can freshen up and rest?" I nodded and Ryan went back to the car to grab our things before we headed inside. Mommy sat down in her chair next to Daddy's. "What did you think of him, Daniel?"

~~~

Daniel grabbed Sarah's hand. He couldn't even look her in the face. "I don't like what I felt when I shook his hand, Sarah. He didn't have the handshake of a man, a *real* one, and that worries me. We have to protect our baby girl."

~~~

Later that night, I found myself standing in the backyard looking at the stars. My fingers cupped around a glass of Mommy's orange lemonade. My mind was flooded with questions. Could I fulfill Daddy's desire for grandchildren? Were Ryan and I really made for each other? Did Ryan's family *really* like me? Who is Kelly?

Prayerfully, everything would work out somehow. God always brings things together in His own way. *I wonder if by this time next year I'll be married and have a baby? Will God let Daddy live long enough to see it?* I paused to take a sip of my drink and let the familiar combination of sweet and sour linger for a moment.

I remembered how sometimes I would go on Facebook and see classmates getting married or having children. I'd see the engagement and the maternity photoshoots. The shots of the ring after the proposal. Some of the girls *severely* needed a good gel refill before taking those shots. The little "Outfits of The Day" that they'd put on their kids. First day of school pictures. It didn't really phase me all that much. Now…here I was beating myself up for putting my career at the forefront of my life. I never used to regret my choice. In a way I still don't, but now Daddy's desire nags me. I used to watch how my friends behaved when they got in their relationships. Some of them made decisions that I questioned. I couldn't see myself changing myself for any man. Yet, here I stand reordering my priorities.

In the beginning, my relationship with Ryan was cute. I wasn't really sure where it would go. I just wanted to have some fun. Then the more I got to know him, the more I realized that I wanted to build a future with him. Ryan set my soul on fire in so many ways. It wasn't lustful or anything like that. He gelled so well with me. The more I learned about him, the more familiar he felt. Even though he had some things here and there that I didn't like, no one is ever perfect in a relationship. I began to accept those little things as quirks. Not like they were doing me any harm in any way. The days I woke up to his smile, the days I would lay in his arms and listen to his heartbeat, it was paradise. He made me feel safe. I felt desired and sexy. Yet, he made me feel something that no one else ever made me feel. Ryan made me feel *seen*. When my heart was broken over a situation or I was angry, he made me feel valid. I could be vulnerable with him. I could trust him with my heart. As fast as everything was going, I knew that Ryan had to be the *one*. Cliché as that thought was, it was true. I had relationships that lasted years and none of them came even remotely close to making me feel this way.

There was one day where I was sitting at my kitchen table and a thought hit me out of nowhere. *What would our child be like?* I envisioned our daughter's beautiful face. I imagined raising her up to be anything she wanted to be in the world. I imagined us raising our son to be a good man like his father. I could see his handsome, little face so clearly. I pictured Christmas and family dinners. I saw, in my mind's eye, Daddy holding his grandchildren. I could see it all as clear as day. Although these weren't my dreams before, in that very moment, I wanted a family with Ryan

Ryan was the one for me and there was no debate about it. I was finally getting the love I deserved. I was finally allowing myself to *be* loved. I had never felt this happy in my life. Feelings are fickle. But this was more than a feeling. It was a state of just being. (That's what Anita advised me to do – just be.) It was a beautiful surprise. Ryan had this presence that was unmistakable. When he went on business trips, I missed him so much. But I didn't just miss him. I missed the feeling of being able to call him from the other room and hearing his voice or having him appear next to me. He gave me comfort. I felt like God designed him just for me.

A soft touch pulled me out of my thoughts. I looked over to see Mommy's tender, sparkling eyes looking at me. Her expression was warm. A small smile sat on her face. I went to speak when I caught the sight of sadness in her eyes. I wondered if something was on her mind about Daddy. She raised a glass of her famous elixir to her lips, taking a few sips. On lowering her glass, she raised her head to look up at the stars. It made me think of the days when she and Daddy would take me "camping" in our backyard. The days of shooting stars, s'mores, and warm fires were so long ago. Still, they felt like yesterday. Fireflies danced their way around the moonlit yard. Mommy was quiet for a while. Wordlessly, she reached out for my hand and held it. When she finally did speak, her voice was as light as the breeze strolling by. "How are you feeling, baby?"

"I should be asking you that, Mommy."

"And here I am beating you to the punch."

"Well, I'm feeling a lot of things, Mommy. It's so much. Like, work has been stressing me out a bit. I'm thinking about possibly stepping out and starting my own firm. That was Ryan's idea, actually. And Ryan…oh my God, Mommy, he's just perfect. I didn't realize how much I wanted a family of my own until he came along." Mommy's face darkened as I spoke. "What's wrong?"

She squeezed my hand tightly, "Honey, I don't think he's the one for you."

My heart stopped, "What, why?! We just got here and things went so well at dinner. Does Daddy feel the same way too?" She stared at her half-empty glass and swirled the remaining juice around without a word. "Why?"

"Brooke, there are things that a parent just knows. We may not always be able to explain it, but we see it. We just want to make sure that you are kept from the thing that can hurt you before you find out the hard way what it is."

I couldn't believe it. Ryan was the first person I brought home to my parents in years. To not have their support rocked my world. How could they come to that kind of conclusion after just a day?

"You guys just have to get to know him, Mommy. Trust me. He's not a bad person. I know you two don't want to see me hurt, but Ryan would never hurt me. Honest."

"Brooke, what was one of the things that I told you after you started dating that one boy in high school?"

"Love is great, but it can make you foolish…"

"That's right. A person could have a good head on their shoulders until a bite from the love bug makes all that sense go out the window. Honey, you don't see how you act when you're with him. You're mesmerized by him. You dote on him. It's clear that *you're* into *him*. He seems like *he's* into *him* too."

"HOW CAN YOU SAY THAT!?! YOU JUST MET HIM!" I was fighting back tears.

A beat passed, "Do you know him well enough to be raising your voice at your own mother?" She let me chew on that question before continuing. "He's changing you, Brooke. It's okay to love and love hard. But don't lose yourself in the process. At the table you were talking about things that never left your mouth before. I gave birth to you. I know you. For you to suddenly come out of nowhere and say maybe you want to take an extended leave from the firm to start a family? You can have a family and still balance your career."

"Oh, right. So, I should wait even longer to have kids? Should I wait for my eggs to shrivel up or should I

70

wait for Daddy to die? Please tell me how balancing my career will help?"

At that point I knew I cut her to her core. Her expression is still etched into my mind. Mommy threw her hands up as if to surrender. A dark cloud of regret was now hanging in the air between me and my mother. "Mommy, I'm sorry-,"

She held up a hand to stop me. "All I'm saying, Brooke, is to take your time and don't rush blindly into it. You won't be able to get any years you lose or waste back. Make sure that if you choose to change your whole life, the person you're changing for is worth it, and he's making some changes for you too." Mommy turned on her heel and began to walk back toward the house.

"Mommy, wait...I'm sorry. It's just a lot of pressure. I worry about Daddy and I just...I don't know."

Mommy didn't even turn to look at me, "I know you're worried about your father, Brooke. But don't let his circumstance short-circuit God's plan for your life. At the end of the day, Daniel will be happy if you're happy." With that, she went into the house. I looked up at the stars again. I don't know what I was looking for. Maybe a shooting star? As if a star has jurisdiction over God's will. I sighed and turned to go back in the house. My eyes went up to the guest room window upstairs where Ryan was sleeping. *I hope he didn't hear any of that, Jesus.*

Fast forward a few days, things were still awkward between me and Mommy. I tried not to project that onto Daddy. And, I really wanted to make sure Ryan didn't get a sense that things were off. His parents liked me; I didn't think it was fair. On this particular morning, Daddy and Ryan went to the lake for some male bonding. I was hoping that their time together would convince Daddy at least that what he and mommy were feeling was wrong. I tried talking with Mommy again, but she wouldn't hear anything of it.

~~~

Out on the Lake

Meanwhile, Ryan was having his own troubles trying to talk to Daniel. Sitting back-to-back on Daniel's aged, green boat, the two sat in silence watching their respective poles for the rare tug of a bite. The fish may not have been biting, but the tension in the air was. It was calm on the lake. The waves gently cradling the boat in their arms. The sun was high in the noon sky, its light painting beautiful, glistening strokes on the water. The chirps of cicadas harmonized with Blue Jays warbling in the distance. The stillness of the moment was disturbed when Ryan cleared his throat in an attempt to clear the air. "So…Mr. Rivers, I wanted to continue the conversation that we started in the car. Brooke is an absolutely phenomenal woman. She has brought so much out of me as a man. She really upgraded me; you know? I thought I was hot stuff before her, but boy was I wrong. I wanted to know if you'd give me your blessing to marry Brooke?"

Suddenly, Ryan's line was greeted by a hard tug. Turning to see the commotion, Daniel let out a soft, tired laugh at the sight of Ryan scrambling to wind his line quick enough. Ryan was exposed, it was easy to see that he never caught a fish in his life, let alone had the patience for it. Daniel's analytical nature took in every second. The fish escaped and angrily Ryan threw down his fishing pole. Daniel shook his head at the display, "You know son, success will elude you if you don't have the character to keep it."

Ryan was caught off guard by Daniel's matter of fact quip. "I'm sorry sir, what does character have to do with fishing or success?"

Daniel didn't miss a beat, "I was young once, so I understand the pressure of meeting someone's parents for the first time. Sarah's parents weren't too excited about me back then. I was determined to prove them wrong. You might have swept Brooke off of her feet, but as a man and as her father, I'm apprehensive. I want the best for my daughter. She's my only child and she deserves the best in the world. I'm not sure how much more time the good Lord will give me. But I do know this; so long as I have breath in my body, I will not let someone mistreat my pride and joy." Daniel paused to place a hand on Ryan's shoulder, his grip still firm in his weakened state. "Ryan, if you can give me your word, as a man, and show me proof that you're capable of doing everything in your power to take good care of Brooke; then Sarah and I will give you our blessing on those conditions. I hope I've answered the question you wanted to ask me, you know, before the fish on your line got away."

Ryan silently nodded his head and turned his back to Daniel, slowly becoming dejected about not only losing the fish, but potentially losing Brooke as well. Ryan could only sit in his feelings for so long before Daniel started a nasty coughing fit. After handing Daniel a bottle of water Ryan said, "Come on Mr. Rivers, let's get you home."

~~~

When Daddy and Ryan came back, I noticed that Ryan wasn't his usual bubbly self. He was more reserved as he brought a tired Daddy into the house. By then, it was time for dinner. I felt on edge the whole time we were sitting at the table. Every fiber of my being wanted to find a reason to excuse myself so I could run away. I felt so out-of-body and uncomfortable. I grabbed my fork and quickly shoved a glob of mashed potatoes in my mouth.

Ryan leaned over and whispered in my ear, "Are you okay?" I gave a low mm-hm so I didn't draw my parents' attention to our whispering at the table. Suddenly, Ryan stood to his feet, "I have something I would like to say." Mommy, Daddy, and I all sat there startled by his sudden outburst. None of us could tell where this was headed. Ryan paused to clear his throat. "I'm sorry, I know this is very sudden and this week was the very first time that you've met me. But there's something I'd like to say. I know, as parents, your first instinct is to protect your daughter. I just want to say that I'm absolutely madly and deeply in love with Brooke. She brings so much into my life and I never knew love could be like this until I met her. I hope that over time that you'll trust me with her heart. I would never dishonor your daughter…"

I was stunned… What was Ryan saying? What was he doing? There couldn't have been a more inopportune time for a proposal – at least that was where he seemed to be heading. Everything was happening so fast. I had no idea what Mommy might say and I didn't want Daddy upset – especially on Ryan's first visit. I had to do something to stop Ryan. With food in my mouth, I pulled gently on his shirt tail to get him to sit back down. As I tugged, I was searching my parents' faces to see their reaction. They both had poker faces. He had their undivided attention. I was tugging, searching, and praying.

Please God, let Mommy and Daddy see that things will turn out ok.

Later that night, I found myself sitting on the edge of my bed, letting my eyes chart a path around the room. My parents hadn't changed a thing since I moved out. I caught my reflection in the vanity mirror. The cool and confident expression that usually crowned my face was nowhere to be found. Left in its place was confusion and frustration. My mind kept replaying the tape from dinner. *Of all the times to propose…why did he…?* The thoughts trailed off in the air, leaving the stillness of the moment hanging in suspense. The gnawing, itching feeling creeping in my throat made me feel like I was suffocating. I couldn't find the voice to verbalize what happened. I thought that I was heading for something that was really going to make me happy. Now…I was feeling anything but that. The sound of my bedroom door opening snapped me out of my thoughts. I turned to see Ryan slink through the doorway.

"Ryan, what are you doing in here?" hurt and venom were intertwined in my question. He strode over to my bed wordlessly, attempting to steal a kiss as he sat down. I pushed him away in disgust. "Answer me, Ryan!"

He scoffed, "What? Am I not allowed to see you now?"

"It's not that," I spit back, "You know better than to disrespect my parents in their own house."

"How am I being disrespectful?" I had a hard time reading the look on his face. "It's not like we're two teenagers, Brooke. Plus, it's not like we're doing anything." He reached out to cup my face. I wanted to keep pushing him away, but I could feel myself weakening at his touch. My eyes began to blur from the slowly pooling tears.

Soft lips kissed the center of my forehead. "That's not what I mean, Ryan. I just-I just can't understand how you could do that. What was that stunt you pulled at the family table? Was that some kind of proposal? Don't I deserve something with a little more effort? You probably didn't even ask for my parents' blessing, did you?"

Ryan's eyes fell to the floor, "That's the thing..." I tried the best I could to mentally prepare for what he was about to tell me. "When I went fishing with your dad," he started to nervously turn away from me, "we spent a lot of time talking about you. Your dad wanted to know more about us and I shared what he asked. I told him how much you brought to my world. And then..." His back was now completely turned to me.

"And then what? Ryan, what's going on? Tell me." I pulled at his sleeve to force him to face me.

"I'm not even sure I should say anything, Brooke."

A pain shot through my heart. I closed my eyes as a million scenarios suddenly sped through my mind. "And then what, Ryan? Tell me. Please."

"Brooke, forget I even said anything okay?"

"THAT'S NOT FAIR RYAN!" I could feel the heat rushing in my face. One of the things that I hated more than anything was being left in the dark to play guessing games.

"You don't have the right to build me up and then all of a sudden 180° on me. That's not fair. If it's really something you want to tell me, then be a man and say it."

Ryan's face was twisted into a sheepish expression. "I don't think your parents like me, Brooke. It's like I'm no good for them no matter what I do. Especially when it comes to your dad. When we were on the lake, he expressed that he thought we were moving too fast in our relationship. I just…I don't know, Babe. Things went so well with my parents. I just don't get it."

Now, the sullen look that Ryan and Daddy had when they came back from their fishing trip made sense. Ryan's voice became garbled in my ears and I zoned out. I've been grappling with Daddy's cancer, the pressures at work, and coming to terms with my feelings about Ryan. I felt as though I was suffocating and I thought I was going to pass out. I don't remember what happened next. What I do remember was coming to in Ryan's arms, his sweater was completely soaked from my tears. The stress of the situation was too much for me. I was tired of walking on eggshells for everyone. It felt as though every choice I made caused someone to question me. I just want the people I love to love each other.

Through the haze in my head, I heard Ryan continue, "I asked him for his blessing and he said not yet. He said, 'Young man, you and Brooke are in too much of a hurry. You're not ready to take a wife while you're still figuring out your life. Brooke loves your potential. Sarah and I will applaud your progress. You can have our blessing when we see that you're ready, and you've met our conditions.' I tried to convince him, Babe. I really tried. But because he's so stubborn. I didn't want him taking my determination as disrespect for his rules. So, I backed off."

I couldn't fix my mouth to speak. Numb wouldn't even begin to describe what I felt. I gave into my heartbreak, softly sobbing in Ryan's arms until I fell asleep.

I woke up in a daze. The hazy sky outside of my window matched the cloudiness in my head. I found myself completely alone in my room. Ryan was nowhere to be found. *Did I dream last night?* I looked down and saw that I was in my pajamas. I reach up to feel if my bonnet was on my head. I could feel that my hair was wrapped underneath. *I don't remember putting these on.*

Did I do my hair? What happened? I changed out of my pajamas and went to the bathroom, hoping a quick splash of water on my face would wake me up, it didn't.

The smell of buttery pancakes and sizzling sausage called me from downstairs. *Does Mommy share Daddy's feelings? Has she been holding back from me this whole visit?* I shook the thought out of my mind, praying to God that Ryan's news about Daddy was really a nightmare.

Time seemed to move slowly as I headed down the stairs. The floor below seemed to go further away from me with every step. The sound of Mommy's humming could be heard from the kitchen. The choice of song was all too familiar and way too ironic. Mommy always played Smokey Robinson and The Miracles on the days she would do a full clean of the house. "Shop Around" was one of her favorites. I remember her sitting me down to talk about *the birds and the bees* as a young girl and how she used the song to teach me. Of course, through a more gender appropriate remix, *"Just because you've become a young woman now. There's still some things that you don't understand now. Before some boy asks for your hand now, keep your freedom for as long as you can now. Oh Brookie-baby, you better shop around."*

Reminiscing on that brought me back to the argument that I had with her a few days ago. Mommy went on about her business, completely unaware of my presence. I gently knocked on the wall so I wouldn't startle her as she cooked. She did a double take over her shoulder.

"Brookie-baby, you're up," it didn't matter how old I got, I was still her Brookie-baby. "How'd you sleep?"

I shrugged, "I don't know, Mommy. It feels like I didn't sleep at all. I just feel, tired."

"Sit down, baby." I made my way to the kitchen table. Mommy's eyes were comforting, yet tinged with sadness as she watched me take my seat. She quickly spun around to grab a plate from out of the cabinet. The plate was quickly covered with love: pancakes, sausage, scrambled eggs, French toast with my favorite jam, and corned beef hash.

"Mommy, you know I can't eat all this. I'll ruin my diet." I mindlessly played with the hash in the corner of my plate.

"Hush! You can diet all you want when you get back to Greenwich. Right now, you're at home."

I asked her in a whisper why Daddy didn't think Ryan and I were ready to get married and if she felt the same way. She answered me in a soft voice because we were both well aware how sound carries through the house.

"Daniel was hit with the same feeling I had when we first met him. I can't fully explain it. But your daddy was once his age, and knows how a man that age thinks very well."

I thought back to what else Ryan said last night. "Is that why Daddy gave Ryan conditions?"

"Most likely."

"But Mommy, Ryan is really, really a good guy. You have to believe me."

"Sweetie, the Word says, 'Don't stir up or awaken love until it's ready.' Marriage is not like dating. When you date and things go wrong, it's so much easier to break away than it is when you're in a marriage. A marriage is a covenant, a binding one. When a couple says, ''til death do us part,' you have to make sure that you both really mean it. Remember I told you, don't use your daddy's condition as a crutch for your decision. Even if he were to go tomorrow, he wouldn't want to watch you being miserable while he's in heaven. I think you should give this more time so you can see Ryan for who he really is. Your daddy and my worst fear is you telling that man and his potential yes, and then he slows down his progress because he has you where he wants you. If he wants to be a pastor, wait until he gets a church. I need you to hear me, baby. Just because a man proposes to you doesn't mean that you have to say yes. Give yourself some time. There will be other prospects. *I promise.*"

I hung my head. Mommy cupped my head in her hands, "Brooke, I am about to teach you the most powerful prayer I ever prayed. 'Lord, if this is not Your will for my life, shut it down.' If it's His plan for you, then He will do whatever it takes to make it come to pass. But if this isn't of Him, honey take the first sign He gives you and run the other way." I gave her a weak smile.

That night, I whispered a prayer in my heart as I was trying to sleep. I wanted to pray the shutdown prayer. But each time I thought about it, I was struck with fear. I had already started picturing Ryan as the father of my children and Daddy being so pleased with grandchildren. Besides, I knew in my heart that God made Ryan just for me. *Right?*

A few more days went by. It seemed like every waking moment that Ryan spent every effort to wait on me hand and foot, so long as he was in the same space as Mommy and Daddy. He was doting on me. Did he hear what Mommy said that first night? Or, was he overcompensating because of their reservations about him? About us moving too fast? Maybe he was just burning off nervous energy. Who knows? Mommy and Daddy had a whirlwind romance. Why can't we? Daddy proved Mommy's parents wrong. So, Ryan can prove mine wrong too. I felt like a Stretch Armstrong toy being pulled in different directions.

Chapter 9

Private & Public Proposals

One sunny afternoon, Ryan took me to Rainbow Falls for a brunch date for two. The farther we drove from the house, the freer I felt. No pressure to be Daniel and Sarah's good little girl. I hadn't even realized how much I'd been suppressing my grown and sexy side. My peach sundress gracefully hugged my curves. I was in my element; divine and feminine. I was so enraptured by the bliss of escaping my parents' gaze that I was overwhelmed by the sight and sound of the cascading waterfalls. The roar was relaxing and exhilarating at the same time. They truly lived up to their name. When the sunbeams kissed the falls, bands of color could be seen dancing between them.

Ryan must have asked for my favorite brunch basket at the bistro in town: fresh fruit, with a charcuterie board featuring the best Jamón Ibérico de bellota, black truffle salami, honey, and Brie, paired with a bottle of White Arneis. He picked the perfect spot, away from the traffic of the trail. The early afternoon air was crisp, but I was warmed by our pleasant conversation. After we finished our meal, Ryan and I sat in silence listening to the falls for a while. I lay back to watch the clouds as they lazily rolled by. Out of the corner of my eye, I noticed that Ryan was still sitting up and he had an oh so familiar smirk on his face. I raised a brow as if to ask, *What are you thinking?*

Ryan slightly scooted back the slit of my dress until it reached my bikini line, leaving my right leg completely bare. Sunlight glittered across my skin. I sat up a little, curious, still trying to figure out what he was going to do. He pulled off the sandal of my exposed leg and began to caress and massage my foot. He alternated between pressing, kneading, and squeezing; his thumb seemed to walk across a path that it knew all too well. He took great care with each tender press and stroke. I could feel myself beginning to melt in his hands. As I relaxed, he motioned for me to give him my other foot. I happily obliged, letting him remove my other sandal. His hands performed a show-stopping encore. I was floating on a cloud of ecstasy. Ryan's loving was dangerously calculated and analytical. He was never done when you thought he was and he always had a trick up his sleeve.

Grabbing the bottle of honey, he drizzled a path along my inner leg. A path of kisses danced downwards, closer and closer to his goal, until my conscious reminded me of where we were.

"Ryan," my tone an exasperated whisper because he was just getting to the good part. "You know we can't do this here. We're in *public*."

He paused. His gaze lifted to meet mine without his lips leaving their post. There was a voracious hunger in his eyes. He rebelled against me, continuing to kiss higher until he reached my inner thigh, never breaking eye contact with me. He stopped again, squeezed my thigh, and began to alternate between kissing and nibbling it. He watched me fail horribly at resisting the urge to squirm. I bit back my protests because I was afraid of someone potentially coming to investigate the noises I wanted to make. *"Brooke, Brooke, Brooke…"* the coolness in his voice had me on edge. "Do you really think I did all this work to find a spot like this for someone to see us? Where we are is nowhere near the path everyone takes. Even if someone were to come up this way from the main campgrounds, it would take them a little over an hour by car. So, you could imagine how much longer it takes on foot. That is, unless you still want to wait until after we're married?"

I imploringly nodded my head yes. Having him rev my engine that much was SUCH a tease. Ryan smiled at the sight of me almost begging and returned to massaging my legs. His fingers finished the dance his lips had begun. I fell adrift at the sensations of his touch.

My body hummed in the afterglow. Ryan, wrapped himself around me. His face said that he was extremely proud of himself. There was never a dull moment with him. I could feel a nap coming on when suddenly, I had an idea. "How about a nice game of Acey Deucey?" We played that version of backgammon so much that the board was in the car.

"Acey Deucey!?! You have the energy for that right now?" he grinned showing all of his pearly whites.

"Hush. I've been invigorated! So…let's make a bet," I teased.

Ryan's ears perked up, "A bet?" He smiled coyly and bit his lip, "What are you proposing?"

"Well," I pushed my hair behind my ear, "Funny you should use that terminology. The loser has to be the one to convince my parents that we're ready for marriage."

That sheepish expression returned to Ryan's face. "Seriously, Brooke?"

It may have been the wine, but I was in a teasing mood. "You're not scared of a little challenge, are you?"

Flashing that smile I loved, he took my hand and kissed it. "I'd do anything to win you."

"Good, then let's play." I chirped as he went running back to the car to grab the board.

It may have been mischievous of me to make such a bet. But we had to do something to get everybody on the same page. In Greenwich, I was sure my parents would love Ryan. And I wasn't going to let the stress of this situation steal my joy. After I won, I may or may not have gloated at the thought of Ryan having to work harder to win over my parents. I stared at the rainbows in the falls thinking, somehow, someway, this was going to work.

Ryan softly tucked a finger under my chin, drawing my gaze back to him. "Marry me," he proposed.

"Hmmm, what's your hurry young man?" I joked in Daddy's voice. Ryan pouted at my playful jab.

"Don't you love me?" His question accompanied by puppy dog eyes.

"I do."

"Then say yes, so 'I do' can be our reality." I took his hand from under my chin and kissed it before cuddling up to him. We sat in silence for a while, listening to the music of the falls. I could feel myself getting sleepy as I was wrapped in Ryan's warmth. The smell of his cologne was soft and drawn out by our natural surroundings. I was trying to fight the urge to sleep, but the peacefulness of the moment was like a blanket.

"Let's pack up so we can go home." Ryan's voice was reassuring. Home…that's where the heart is right? On the drive home, the two of us joked about how Ryan was going to make this work. I wanted my parents to see him as I did. He wasn't a knight in shining armor because I wasn't a damsel in distress. Ryan comforted my soul and complimented my being. No one is perfect, and I know my parents only want the best for me. As Ryan rattled off ideas, one of which was a grandiose musical number, I whispered a silent prayer in my heart that this would work. I nodded off to the sounds of Luther Vandross and Cheryl Lynn playing on the radio:

If this world were mine, I'd place at your feet all that I own; you've been so good to me. If this world were mine, I'd give you the flowers, the birds and the bees. For with your love inside me, that would be all I need. If this world were mine. I'd give you anything...

I woke up to Ryan carrying me into my bedroom. I could hear Mommy asking if I was okay. Ryan said something along the lines of I took one of my famous naps on the drive back. I kept my eyes closed the whole time. I didn't want them to know I was awake and that I could hear them. Ryan gently placed me on the bed and draped his jacket over me as a blanket. The tender touch of a soft kiss on my forehead was the last thing I remembered before drifting back to sleep.

On the last day of our time with Mommy and Daddy, he decided to surprise us all with a trip to The Capital Grille in Charlotte. Compared to our previous dates, he went all out for this one. We were dining in a *Michelin Star* establishment. Ryan pleasantly surprised me; there wasn't a single coupon, nor did he pick the homiest or cheapest of dishes on the menu. He covered all of our meals. It seemed Ryan was more prepared this time around. The restaurant was in a low murmur. A soft ping of a phone had reached my ears.

"I think that's mine," Ryan said, pulling out his phone slightly from his pocket. Excitedly, Ryan got up from the table and gave me a kiss on the forehead, "I'll be right back." He vanished too quickly for me to ask where he was going. Daddy occasionally winced, trying to remain in good spirits for the rest of us. I hated seeing him in pain more than anything. Mommy and I perused the dessert and wine menus, I couldn't help but wonder where Ryan had run off to.

~~~

Ryan excitedly scrolled through the message he received at the dinner table:

Greetings and salutations in the strong name of Jesus Christ. Rev. Black, I would like to personally thank you for your interest in the pastoral position here at Bountiful Harvest Church. Your resume left a strong impression on our council. The need for a follow up was virtually unanimous. We would like to set up some time for you to come in for an interview to see if our humble church and your leadership are compatible as it is imperative that our visions of ministry are able to successfully marry. Please call our secretary to set up your interview appointment. God bless you and we're looking forward to meeting you.

Regards, Elder Tony Franklin

~~~

Mommy and I were happily enjoying a slice of cheesecake when out of the blue, I heard a familiar voice breakthrough the hum of the dining room, "Ladies and gentlemen, may I have your attention please?" I looked up to my left. Once again, Ryan was making a scene at the table. *Lord, did You have to make the man fine **and** ghetto?*

"I hate to interrupt your evening, but I want to acknowledge someone very special." The dining room fell into a hush. Eyes upon eyes looked at us. I wasn't sure if I would die of the embarrassment or the attention first. A few of the snow bunnies at the table to the side of us appeared to be getting their phones ready. My mind anxiously scrambled through scenarios. The world once again sounded garbled and I couldn't bring myself to look Mommy and Daddy in the face. I could feel Ryan's hand pulling me up to stand.

"My dearest Brooke, when God created the universe and all that was in it, He left a bit of heaven on earth. That bit of heaven was you. I have never known a woman so kind, so loving, so wonderful, so amazing, and so hardworking. I love that you're a dreamer and that you're a goal-getter. You're independent, yet you still respect me as a man. You love and you love hard. Each day, I find myself falling further and further in love with you. The future I envision with you is a grand one. I couldn't dream of building the life that I want to build without you.

"Now that it's official that I'm going to become a bishop at Bountiful Harvest Church, I couldn't imagine leading without you by my side. I can't be Bishop Black without you as my First Lady. You understand me. You go above and beyond to meet me where I am. I catch myself smiling like a fool when I think of your smile. I'm smitten by the sound of your laugh. My heart beats a song that I hope you hear. I can't imagine living in a world without you or your love. I hope that, as a Bishop, I have proven to your parents that I can love and provide for you in the ways that you deserve. You are my soulmate and I want to give you every single part of me. In the words of Jagged Edge," Ryan then turned to a server and made a gesture as if he was supposed to be handed something. I quickly took my seat as the nervous waiter scampered up with a microphone. Ryan held the microphone at chest level. My mind went full NeNe Leakes…*The ghetto, the ghetto, THE GHETTO.*

Ryan inhaled sharply, "*Meet me at the altar in your white dress,*" After that first line, I was twisting in my seat like Ryan was one of The Five Heartbeats. "*We ain't getting no younger, we might as well do it. Been feeling you all the while girl I must confess. Girl let's just get married. I just wanna get married.*" Ryan got down on bended knee and pulled out a beautiful diamond and sapphire ring. The tension was tight in the air. I wanted to look at Mommy and Daddy in hopes that they would be smiling. But I couldn't bring myself to. Everyone around the room seemed to be leaning on the edge of their seat. One of the snow bunnies holding her phone at the table seemed to be recording everything that was happening. I could feel my chest heaving. I gave into my heart and looked back at Mommy and Daddy.

God…please…

Chapter 10

With You, I Thee Wed

I fumbled with the lace of my dress. I could barely breathe and it wasn't because of my corset. My eyes kept going to the clock. *11:58...11:58.* There was a buzz about today. I looked out of my window as my girlfriends posed for pictures outside in their matching lilac dresses. *Something old, something old...Mommy's veil.* I couldn't believe it. Brooke Rivers, the Brooke Rivers was about to get married. I never thought I'd see the day. *Something new, something new...my necklace.* I kept going back to my mirror. I was paranoid, constantly fixing this one hair that did everything in its power to not stay in place. *Something borrowed, something borrowed...Ella's pin.* I was fidgeting with my veil every five seconds. At one moment I loved it, the next, I hated it. *Something blue... my ring.*

"Knock knock! Are you almost ready?" The question was followed by the slow creak of my bedroom door opening. Two familiar faces popped around it, my besties Tina and Yvette.

"Ready as I will ever be," I answered.

My breath was trying to get stuck in my throat. The pair entered the room, followed by excited squeals and exclamations. Tina, my maid of honor, swooped in to give me a hug, only to stop and tuck the annoying hair behind my ear. At least someone was able to slay my frizzy foe. Yvette had planned the ceremony with Tina's help. "Only the best for members of the first and finest Sorority." That was her motto from the very beginning. Only the best entertainment. Only the best wine. Only the best church. The best! The best! The theme was "Our Love" after the Natalie Cole song.

> *Our love will stand tall as the trees. Our love will spread wide as the seas. Our love will shine bright in the night like the stars above. And we'll always be together, our love.*

I was still in shock. I remembered how I was so lost in my ambitions that I thought this day would never come. But everything changed when Ryan entered my world. Love came fast, whisking me away into a world that I had never known.

"You look good, girl." Tina said as she looked me up and down. She inspected my dress for any flaws and was ready to help me hike up the dress to use the bathroom. "You look like a princess." The thought made me smile. Ever since Ryan, it was like I had entered a fairy tale.

Yvette echoed Tina's sentiment in her own humorous way. *"SHE'S YOUR QUEEEEENNNN TO BE!"* Tina playfully gave her a smack. "Okay, okay. I'll stop." She looked up at the clock. "Oh! It's 12:00. We gotta go. We don't want to hit traffic. You only get married for the first time once, you know."

I looked in the mirror one more time. *Is my veil crooked?* I reached up a hand to fix it again, only for Tina to grab it, "Girl it's fine. Let's go!" She hurried me out of the room so she could begin her duties of making sure my train didn't drag. The limo ride was a hoot. My girls were singing their hearts away to Mariah Carey, Toni Braxton, and some of our other favorite divas. The playful noisiness helped to distract me from the butterflies swarming my stomach. I couldn't have asked for a better day. The sun was bright. Not a cloud in the sky. It was a perfect springtime wedding.

When we arrived at the church, my bridesmaids went into secret agent mode, doing everything in their power to make sure Ryan didn't see me before the ceremony. My bridal escort was successful, having gotten me to my bridal chambers without a hitch. My maids left me to handle last-minute touches before the wedding started. The sudden solitude had left me slightly unsettled. It was the dawning realization that these were the last few moments that I would be single. I looked out the window, watching as guests slowly began to file in. Ryan's mother and stepfather were among the first to arrive. Ella's dress slightly bordered on upstaging mine, but thankfully, it wasn't white. I decided to take a seat before my anxiety could get to me.

I hummed to myself, gently rocking back and forth in my chair. I wanted to be excited. At the same time, I felt like everything around me was ready to crash on top of me. Was I getting cold feet? I thought about Mommy and Daddy. I wondered how they felt about me moving forward with this. I hoped that Ryan had won them over since the night of his very public proposal. I just wanted us to be a happy family. *Knock Knock.* The sound was delicate on the door. "Come in," I called. I was greeted by the familiar smell of rose and vanilla. "MOMMY!"

I sprang up from the chair, almost breaking my neck to get to her.

"Whoa! Slow down, Brookie-baby. Don't hurt yourself on a big day." It felt so good to hug her. There was nothing like a mother's hug to remind you that things were going to be okay. "You look beautiful."

Mommy looked so tiny standing next to me as I towered over her in my heels. I searched her eyes for her wisdom. I could see on her face that she was tired. I knew it wasn't easy trying to take care of herself and Daddy. Her black and grey tweed dress seemed to swallow up her small frame.

"Mommy, have you been eating?"

"Yes, I have. This dress is about as old as you." The wrinkles on her face echoed her smile. "As a matter of fact, I was probably carrying you the last time I wore it."

I shook my head and laughed, "So long as I don't have to worry about you."

"Now, now," she chirped, "That's me and your daddy's job."

"Speaking of, where is Daddy?"

"He's seated already. Ryan met us at the car and helped Daniel get inside."

"Is he okay with you walking me down the aisle in his place?"

"Well, he's as okay as he can be."

I lowered my head, fighting back tears.

"No, baby. I know he wanted to do this. But he's okay. We just want to support you on your special day."

"Thank you, Mommy. I love you."

"I love you too," Mommy paused after something caught her eye. "You're wearing my veil. You know, the day I married your father was the best day of my life. Your grandmother made me this veil from the fabric of her wedding dress. It's our own little family heirloom. I hope that you'll be able to pass this to your daughter should God bless you with one. I'm proud of you."

I mouthed another word of thanks before giving Mommy one more squeeze. Soon she left me to get into place. Today was bittersweet for a lot of reasons. Seeing Mommy and hearing her confidence gave me the boost I needed. I searched the room for a clock. *1:30. Only half an hour until my life changes forever.* It was only a matter of time before my bridal party returned, ready to help usher me into a new season of life. *"SKEEEWWWW-WEEE!"* they called, supporting me not only as friends, but as my Sorority sisters. I had an army by my side. I could feel the nervousness in me beginning to break. I was going to enjoy this day to the fullest. We left the bridal chamber and made our way downstairs. As we approached the sanctuary, Mommy was nowhere to be found. I happened to see Ryan's best man Michael walking the halls. "Hey Mike, have you seen my mom? She's supposed to be here." Before he could answer me, another voice answered my question.

"She's sitting in the sanctuary," I turned to look in the direction of the voice and lost it. *Daddy.* With cane in hand, he slowly made his way toward me. I wanted to run to him, but he was so frail that I didn't want to hurt him.

"Daddy, what are you doing here?! You should be sitting inside. I thought Mommy was going to walk me." My eyes scanned the hall to see if there was a chair that I could get him.

"This is your big day, Brooke. You are my pride and joy. I wasn't going to miss it for the world. Daddy's here."

I was overwhelmed. There were so many moments that made this day hard to grasp. Slowly but surely, everything was coming together for this to be the day of my dreams. I wouldn't have minded if Mommy was the one to walk me down the aisle. Deep in my heart however, I did want Daddy to do it. I leaned in to hug him, and soak in his warmth.

"Places, everyone!" Yvette called. Tina seemingly pulled a makeup kit out of nowhere to touch up my face before I went inside. There would be no runny mascara on her watch. The bridesmaids, groomsmen and Jessica, the flower girl, had lined up ahead of me and Daddy. I felt joy bubbling up on the inside! The doors opened and my fairytale wedding ceremony began.

White roses and lavender. White lights along the sides of the aisle. A harp sweetly blended with the light plucks of a violin and the deep bellow of a cello. The sanctuary and the guests all fell away as my eyes fell on Ryan. My heart swelled at the sight of him. He looked like a prince in his white suit. This day did not seem real. Cloud nine wouldn't even begin to describe where I was. I was in heaven. Before I knew it, I was looking at Ryan face to face. I could hear my father whisper, "Take care of my little girl, Ryan. Please."
Ryan gave my father a silent nod before returning his

gaze to me. He broke his gaze again to help Daddy to his seat, garnering an "Awwww…" from the guests.

Once Ryan returned to his spot, the pastor began, "Dearly beloved, we are gathered here today…"

Chapter 11

Honeymoon Horrors
Cruise: 1ˢᵗ Night

It wasn't supposed to be like this. Searing hot pain courses through my cheek like a match striking fire against my jawbone. My world is hazy. I feel as though I'm on a turbulent carpet ride passing through a heavy fog. The sea is rough because a storm is rising. A blow strikes the back of my head. A fist crashes into my side. I can barely breathe. I don't recognize the monster beating me. *This was supposed to be the happiest time of my life.* I want to weep, but no sound comes out.

24 Hours Earlier: The Wedding Night

"And now we will have the father/daughter dance!" Yvette proudly shouted into the mic. This whole night had been a fairy tale. I couldn't believe it. I was now Mrs. Brooke Black on paper, but I was still Brooke Rivers in practice. I was slowly getting closer to realizing my dream of having my own firm. I had a husband who loved me and a family who supported me. The whole night there was magic in the air. I felt like I was on top of the world and that I had obtained true happiness. I didn't have everything that I wanted yet. But I was getting close to it. I could have flown from Earth to Pluto and back a million times. I didn't want this moment to end. I didn't have to worry about Daddy's illness or Ryan not getting along with Mommy and Daddy. I didn't have to worry about being rejected for partner. I didn't have a single care in the world. Today was my day and the start of a new forever.

The reception hall was lively. Everyone seemed to have their own glow. Some of my bridesmaids were cutting up with the groomsmen. Ryan was dancing with Mommy. Daddy sat at the table and smiled at the sight. I had a hard time reading the look on his face. It was like he wanted to be happy and enjoy everything like everyone else, but he was so tired. I went over and gave Daddy a hug and a kiss on the forehead. He didn't say anything but gave me a smile and squeezed my hand tight. I could feel the love emitting from his weary bones.

Cruise: 4th Night

SLAM! I find myself locked eye to eye with the monster again. I'm trapped in his clutches. The monster's grip tightens around my throat. I claw at the hand hoping to break free. But there's no use. I'm not strong enough. I'm defenseless. The corners of my eyes become tinged with black. The world begins to blur and spin. My body wants to pass out, but my mind fights to stay awake. I'm fearful of what will happen if I shut my eyes. Claws dig into my neck. The monster's grasp crushes my futile attempts to draw in enough air to scream. Even if I could cry out, there is no one to come to my rescue. We're completely isolated. This was the monster's plan all along; to have me alone.

His breath reeks of the putrid stench of alcohol. It drips from his mouth like venom. Darkness tries again to swallow me up. I find myself contemplating if I should give into it. I'm crumpled up on the floor after being slammed into the wall. The monster is commanding me to get up. But I can't move and I don't want to. The monster repeats his command. I'm paralyzed from fear and heartache. *This wasn't what I was promised.*

The monster tears at my ankle, pulling my leg as if he sought to rip it from the socket. The carpet with its thousand needles reaches up and burns my skin as I'm being dragged across it. I close my eyes. I already know where the monster is taking me and why. I don't want to go. I get the impulse to resist. I think about grabbing the door jam and holding on for dear life. I become afraid again. I hate myself. *Why didn't I see?* I'm dreading what comes next. I'm hoisted up in the air and thrown on the bed like a rag doll. I know what the monster wants. I want to tell him no. I want to fight back. I want to scream at him and tell him that I don't want this. But I stay quiet. God knows what will happen if I do. I lay there, keeping my eyes fixed on the ceiling. I try to count the bumps on it but keep losing count. I feel the weight of the monster on top of me. His ghastly claws grope at me. I don't move. He gets angry. He wants me to respond. I don't have it in me. I keep thinking about my prince and how the monster took him away.

BAM! A fist to the mattress close to my face. I may as well be laying in my casket. His voice bellows with fury. I disassociate. For a moment, it seems like I leave my body. But I'm trapped and forced to watch everything. The monster looks like my prince. He has hands like my prince. But he's not my prince. I watch my face twist, holding back the urge to cry. It's hard seeing him take pleasure in my pain. Eventually, the monster stops his brutal assault. He finishes and rolls over like nothing happened. *I should have listened.*

I lie there curled into a ball, being careful not to sob too loud. I don't want to wake the monster back up. There's nothing but the far-off sounds of the sea, the low hum of the air conditioner, the sound of his breathing, and the static from the TV. Minutes pass as if they were hours. I gather all of the strength that I can muster and crawl toward the bathroom. I have to try to find a way to use the bathroom without screaming in pain.

I give the bathroom door more mercy than I was shown, closing it gently behind me. I place one hand on the cold metal sink in the claustrophobically cramped space and another on the hard plastic toilet. I brace myself for what is to come. *One…two…three…*I force my body to stand. The action of being on my two feet delivers a shock throughout my battered and bruised body. I am once again reminded about the betrayal I'm experiencing. I catch a glimpse of a figure in the mirror. Her face is pallid and sunken in. Her cheek is bruised and hair disheveled. I want to run away, but I know the monster will catch me and bring me back just like he did this time. The figure looks woozy. Is she concussed? How is she going to make herself look normal? She can't stay in this bathroom for the remainder of the cruise, or even in this cabin for that matter. I take a closer look at the figure in the mirror. I realize she's wearing my skin.

Three Months Before the Wedding

I found myself buried in endless wedding catalogs from Yvette. I had to pick my colors, the décor, the dresses, and more. I needed a break. I didn't know that preparing for one of the best days of my life was going to be so stressful. I decided that I was going to go to First Baptist and see if I could catch Pastor Townes in his office. I needed to vent. I needed Jesus. I needed to worship. I needed all the help I could get. I pulled into the church parking lot and saw a familiar face coming from inside. I rolled down my window, "Good morning, Mother Higgins!"

Her head quickly swerved in the direction of my voice. "Oh hey, baby!" Her laugh was delightful, "It feels like I haven't seen you in a month of Sundays. How are you doing?"

"I'm doing well, Mother. This week was a little rough, though. Is Pastor inside?"

She frowned slightly, "Why yes, Brooke. But what's the matter? Can I pray for you?"

What I loved about Mother Higgins was that she wasn't like the usual church mother. If you told her your business she did her best to make sure it stayed between the two of you. Unlike the majority that like to make it the church's business, too. "Yes Mother, you can pray for me." I reached my hand out of the window for her to take it. Her finger grazed over my engagement ring from Ryan and she immediately noticed.

"This is new…it's beautiful. I didn't know you were married, Sugar."

"Not yet, Mother. But that's why I'm here. I've been so stressed planning this wedding that I needed to get some encouragement for my soul."

"Okay, so now I know what to pray for. Do you have a picture of the lucky man?"

I pulled out my phone to show her a picture of Ryan. Her face darkened. "Hmmm…" was all she said.

"Something wrong, Mother?" I valued her opinion but I wasn't about to go through the hoops and hurdles of proving our relationship to anyone else.

Her tone was cautious, "I'm happy for you, Brooke. Just make sure this is the one that God sent and not a counterfeit. Now, don't think I'm picking on you. I say that to everyone. Someone once told me to take 1 Corinthians 13:4-7 and replace the word love with the name of your future spouse. If what you read matches the behavior that you see, then you know you are on the right path. God will always give you signs and back them up with His Word. Trust Him." She squeezed my hand tightly. "Pastor Townes should be in his study or in the sanctuary." I squeezed her hand back and mouthed, "Thank you." Mother Higgins gave me her warm smile, "You'll invite me, won't you?"

"Of course," I said. She gave my hand one more squeeze and then headed to her car. I made sure that she was safe in her car before I went inside. The church was quiet for the most part, save for the choir practicing in the sanctuary. That meant that Pastor Townes must have been in his office. Sure enough, that's where he was. Hunched over his Bible with a furrowed brow, coffee mug in hand, Pastor Townes didn't even notice me standing in the doorway. I waited for him to put down his mug before knocking so I wouldn't startle him. *Knock Knock!*

"Hm? Oh hello, Brooke! I'm sorry I didn't see you there. Come in, come in! What brings you by today?"

I took a seat in the chair in front of his desk. The upholstery was a bit chewed through on the seat. It was itchy when it touched my skin. "Well Pastor Townes, I need advice. I am a few months away from my wedding. I find that I'm having to run here and there to make sure things are done. I'm trying to make sure my family gets along well with my beloved. I have to keep track of who's flying in and who's bringing a plus one. And I still have to balance life on top of that. I just feel drained, Pastor. I don't know what to do. Then I keep having people tell me to make sure that the man I love is the one. I know what God has shown me. So why do I need to prove it to them?"

Pastor Townes peered at me over his glasses. His face was like polished stone, stoic and poised. "Weddings aren't easy to plan. Marriages aren't either. Sometimes we think that God is giving us the go ahead on someone or something and we forget to check our blind spots. So, He will send people that will at least remind you to check them."

"I don't understand, though. My fiancé is a man of God. He's getting ready to lead as Bishop at Bountiful Harvest. He's sweet and kind. He makes me feel like I am loved. I don't know what it is that they're seeing that I'm not."

"Love can make us blind, child. And just because someone is a man of God does not mean that they are without fault. David was a man after God's own heart and still had flaws. Be careful that you don't become offended with God reminding you where the emergency exits are. You don't want to be caught in a fire that you can't escape."

"But Pastor, you've met him! I'm sure that your Spirit discerned that Ryan is a good man."

He took a moment to push back his glasses before using the same hand to reach for his mug again. He took a contemplative sip and sat for a moment. "You're right, Brooke. I did meet him and yes, I discerned. But there are things that are done in plain sight that you don't need the Holy Spirit to see."

"Such as?"

"Character can be very telling Brooke. I don't think he's ready for marriage *or* the pulpit. He has potential for both, but he's still very immature. I'm not saying leave him Brooke. Just remember that seeds don't sprout in the same season they're planted. Take your time, and if he's the man God sent for you, waiting won't be an issue."

Present Day: Nine Months into the Marriage

Can't believe I slept late today. I haven't been sleeping well lately. I'm in so much pain; mentally, physically, and emotionally. What a relief to wake up without Ryan in bed next to me! He must be out for his morning run. I'm exhausted. Can't figure out how I ended up here; relieved to wake up alone when I've only been married nine months.

Everything went wrong on our layover in Florida. There, Ryan got really drunk and kept on drinking. I tried to get him to stop but he became infuriated. He pushed me away violently and said some very hurtful things about me growing up with a silver spoon in my mouth, never having to struggle for anything, always getting everything I wanted handed to me, and not appreciating how hard life is for him. I saw a rage in him that left me terrified. I felt trapped. It was too late for us to break up. We were married.

I started to beat myself up for not listening to the warnings to wait. I couldn't believe he had hidden this part of his personality. I kept asking myself, *Why didn't you listen to the warnings?* I thought about flying back home from Ft. Lauderdale but told myself I was overreacting. I rationalized it was his fear of flying and he would relax once we were in our cabin on the cruise ship. Besides, how would I explain to anyone why I was back so soon? Everyone was at our wedding and would expect me to be on my honeymoon. It would sound crazy to say that Ryan drank too much and turned into someone else. So, I journeyed on to San Juan. Only, he didn't relax on the cruise ship. He unraveled. I was too ashamed to call my parents and tell them that their reservations were right. I couldn't imagine the embarrassment I would experience if I called one of my friends.

Ryan and I agreed early on that we wouldn't *actually* consummate our love until we were on our honeymoon. We did our best to do things God's way so God would bless us as a ministry couple. I thought that night would be magical. But the man I married turned out to be maniacal. On the first night of our honeymoon, when I gently suggested that we get some sleep because he had too much to drink, he retorted that he couldn't and wouldn't wait any longer. Despite his protests, he was flaccid. I playfully pointed out that we had seven days to make love. The enraged man I saw in Ft. Lauderdale returned suddenly and assaulted me for laughing at him. With fists swinging, he kept shouting, "Don't laugh at me!" *Who had I married?*

The next day, Ryan reappeared apologizing profusely. He showed me the rejection email he received from Bountiful Harvest while we were in flight to Florida, said that made him drink the way he did, begged me to forgive him for his outbursts, and promised he would never behave that way again. For the next three days, he doted on me. Waited on me hand and foot. Apologized over and over. Swore it was the alcohol and rejection email. Made me all sorts of promises, only to break them on the fourth night of our seven-day cruise.

The monster and I are now known as Bishop and Lady Black of New Salem Baptist Church in Stamford. I don't really know anyone here. My support network was in Greenwich. I feel isolated and alone. Our new neighborhood is as run down as my spirit. I'm no longer the confident, independent Brooke who once dated and adored Ryan. I want to put out an all-points bulletin for him. Sometimes I fantasize about his return. I imagine he's trapped inside Bishop's body trying to make his way back to me. It's as if the shattering of his Bountiful Harvest dream caused him to have a psychotic break. In my fantasy, I reach him and draw him out by playing Rose Royce's "Love Don't Live Here Anymore."

You abandoned me. Love don't live here anymore. Just a vacancy. Love don't live here anymore. Just emptiness and memories of what we had before.

In the nightmare that is my reality, Bishop is a complete stranger. His foreboding presence makes Sebastian uneasy. We both miss being pampered and spoiled by Ryan. In public, I smile and pretend that I'm enamored with Bishop. Anything less than veneration embarrasses him. This is not the life I envisioned. I keep asking myself what I did to deserve this. I don't understand why God is letting this happen. Why didn't He step in to save me from this monster? He helped Bountiful Harvest dodge the Bishop bullet. I know it's sometimes said that while we're praying for a problem to end, God is already dispatching our solution. I just hope and pray mine gets here quick, fast, and in a hurry. I can't handle much more of this.

Chapter 12

Complexities

Click, Click, Click sang the balls of the Newton's Cradle on my desk. Perfectly balanced and in rhythm with one another. I wish I could say that was how my life felt. It's been two years since Bishop and I tied the knot. I've wanted to untie it since our disastrous honeymoon. But by then, it was already too late. *Click, Click,* the metronome of the Cradle continues in my ears. I look at the clock. It's getting late. I'll have to leave soon. It's Wednesday, time for me to put on another Oscar winning performance. I will be playing the role of *The Good Wife,* a woman who just about sacrificed all of her hopes and dreams for a man she barely loves anymore. *The Good Wife* makes appearances whether she wants to or not because if she doesn't, the scandal would be too great to bear.

Wednesday nights were for Bible Study, something that I once loved was now something I grew to detest thanks to Bishop. I felt like an imposter every time I stepped foot into New Salem. You wouldn't be able to tell if you were looking from the outside in. I hid it in my smile. I hid it in my walk. I hid it under my clothes and with makeup. It was my job to be quiet and look pretty. I was an accessory to Bishop's illusions of grandeur. In his mind, he was the next T.D. Jakes. In my mind, he was T.D. Fake. The sermons he preached every Sunday waxed poetic, but even the devil knows Scripture. I gathered my things, turned the light off in my office, and resentfully made my way to the car.

I sat in the car for a few minutes. The red sunset dimming behind me in my rear-view mirror. I stared at the doors of what would have been my new firm by now if most of my money hadn't ended up being funneled into Bishop's aspirations for New Salem. This marriage not only trapped me mentally and emotionally, but I was also trapped financially. Prior to our wedding, Bishop had talked me into merging our bank accounts. We were going to be sharing a life together, so why not just share our funds? I made the mistake many women are told not to make and trusted him. I wish I could have created a secret separate account. Bishop became aware of how much money I was making and took full advantage of it.

If I happened to treat myself to something he didn't approve of, he would always ask me what I did with the money or yell at me for spending too much of *his* money. It wasn't our money anymore; it was *his* money even though I was making most of it. Even if I tried making another account, he would just grow suspicious of the money going out and where it was. Once I thought about making a run to my parents' house and never coming back. I went to the gas station to fill my tank after work. I was prepared to pack what I could to leave that night. But when I went to put my card in the reader, something told me to check the balance on my phone. Bishop had practically cleaned out the account. Multiple expenses: clothing, alcohol, and props for some of his antics at the church among many other things. I was dejected. My sudden moment of bravery was now stolen from me. I went back in my wallet, took out the little cash I had and put a couple of gallons in my tank. The gauge barely went to half full.

Aside from not being able to break free from Bishop, there was something else that bothered me about that experience. I couldn't place some of the transactions that I saw. It was strange, they were repeated CashApp transactions to the same accounts; KWilson and CMorrison.

The names didn't match any of Bishop's friends that I knew of. But my investigations fell off due to new distractions.

I caught glimpses of the sunset fading into night as I made my drive to the church. Whitney Houston admonished me from the radio. *"Here I sit trying not to cry. Asking myself, 'Why you do this to me?' Oh baby…"* I was tired of living in Heartbreak Hotel. No. It was Heartbreak Home. As much as I hated going through the motions of this façade, it wasn't always bad. After all, Bishop is a gifted teacher and the Word always energizes me. Frustrated as I was with him, there were times where he seemed to really try to make up for his violent temper tantrums. *"Look what you did to me…"* Sometimes I'd come home from work exhausted and he would put on our favorite slow jams, hold me in his arms, and dance with me the whole night.

It's funny, not in a *haha* kind of way, but there were times where I would see glimpses of the man I fell in love with. I would see it in the way he counseled the couples that came to us at church. He would actually defer to me at times and tell people how wise I am, and how blessed he was to have me. Gag me with a spoon. Nevertheless, the advice we would give to struggling couples did not reflect our own troubled marriage. We were their relationship model, not Will and Jada or Beyonce and Jay-Z. They had us in what they thought was real life. To our congregants, our loving marriage was something tangible. They were close enough to see it and touch it. We had the marriage they wanted. It made me laugh and cry, because if they only knew the truth. *"I thought that you were someone who would do me right. Until you played with my emotions and you made me cry..."*

Young ladies waiting for their Boaz would come to me almost every service. They all said virtually the same thing, "Lady Black, I hope I can have a marriage like yours." "Lady Black, how did you know that Bishop Black was the one?" "Lady Black, can you please pray that God will bless me with a husband like yours?" They were statements and requests that mystified me. On one hand, I was glad our example had caused some young women to raise their relationship standards. On the other, I dreaded the thought of any one of these young women suffering in silence like me. With each of them, I would pray the same thing because God knew the truth about Bishop Black, "Father, give this young lady the desire of her heart. Lead her to the one who You so beautifully created to be the best option for her life and purpose.

We bind the strongman and his attempts at confusion. Shut down any man that the enemy sends as a counterfeit. May Your voice be loud and clear above all others. This is Your daughter made in Your image and with whom You are well pleased. Protect her and guide her in all she does. Amen." *"What you do to me. Can't take what you did to me…"*

Driving through Stamford was nothing like driving through Greenwich. While some would be quick to call it the Crown Jewel of Fairfield County, I was often reminded that not everything that glitters is gold. With each trip downtown I would see a city that was as run down as my soul. You could stop at a traffic light and watch the homeless and addicts as they approached various cars and begged for money to get their next meal or next fix. It was sad because in my heart I wanted to help them, but I could barely help myself. I felt powerless. Some of these faces would be regulars at New Salem. They'd come for a warm place to be for a few hours and a hot meal. Bishop hated when they came but he loved using them for photo ops. They were being used as props, just like I was. Bishop had talked about getting into politics for a while. What better way to do so than by creating the narrative of being a man of God that was passionate about his community? Bishop wanted to be seen as a modern-day Nehemiah.

I remember my shock when he suddenly announced at a service last year that he was going to be running for a seat on the city council in the coming election. At the end of the day, Bishop wanted to be known. The more known he became, the better. He was no longer satisfied with the attention from New Salem, he wanted more. I found myself lost in the hum of congratulations that came after. It was enough having to wear the mantle of First Lady, now I had to possibly wear one as a Councilman's wife. At least I couldn't say that being Bishop's wife was predictably boring. I just wished it came with pleasant surprises instead of so many un-welcomed ones.

Bible study that night fell into its usual groove. The church mothers gossiped and gawked in their respective cliques. There was a mother fussing with her child's iPad in the back of the room. A young man could be seen attempting to spit game at one of the sisters that came. He picked a different one every week. The worship team's practice could be heard through the paper-thin walls. Other members chose to keep to themselves as they waited for the study to start.

Deacon Marvin's boisterous laugh could be heard as the young man from earlier now found himself in the grips of a "When I was your age," lecture. Soon Bishop made his grand entrance and the clamoring came to a quiet. Prayer requests and praise reports were raised. A few worship songs were sung. The lesson was taught and then it was time to go home.

Sunday. Wednesday. Sunday. Wednesday. That was the incessant church routine. Occasionally came a Saturday or some other weekday for me to play the role of *The Good Wife*.

From time to time I'd entertain the thought of leaving Bishop, but then he'd do something to pull me back in. It was never something that made me fall back in love. Rather, it was always something that mimicked the idea of being in love. I didn't mind the random getaways or the trips to the beach. Bishop would still show out when taking me to dinner. Thankfully, the coupons from our dating days never made a return. Yet, I found myself longing for the days where those were the only shortcomings that this man had. I wanted that ignorant bliss again. I wanted the life where I knew who I was again. I missed the old me. I missed the old us.

Sometimes, I found myself questioning what could have been if I never met Bishop. Who might I have met if I kept dating around, looking for someone to help me fulfill Daddy's wish for a grandchild? Or, what could have been if I had just listened to Mommy and stayed focused on becoming the most successful entertainment lawyer the world has ever seen? What doors might God have opened for me if I had waited like everyone suggested? I felt as though my rush to marry Ryan was robbing me of the future God intended.

I eventually came to a point where I abandoned the thought of leaving Bishop. Even though I was still in my 30s, I felt like I was past the point of no return of even trying to remarry. Granted not having kids could have been a notch in my favor. But I couldn't handle the thought of going on a date and wondering if they thought something was wrong with me. My pride was so ingrained in my very public marriage that I became anxious whenever I thought about the "d" word. I hadn't listened to the constant, but gentle warnings. I made my bed, I had to lay in it now. I vowed to love Bishop for better or for worse. I kept hoping that the worst of days would eventually come to an end and the better days would begin. I contemplated if Bishop was really a monster or just an insecure little boy trying his best to be a man that had it all. I considered the possibility that his fits were tied to rejection. I wondered if there was anything I could do to make him feel secure enough to stop seeking more and more worldly attention for affirmation. Maybe this was all one big test that he and I had to make it through. The me from five years ago would probably be trying to shake some sense into the me that I had become. I was sinking in a sea of competing emotions that threatened to swallow me whole with each sweeping wave.

With Bishop's run for city council, I found myself thrust into having to adjust to a new normal. It was a tight race, but his charisma and almost omni-presence to the people of Stamford helped to clinch his victory. I had to get used to the requests for interviews and seeing our names in the paper. More photo ops came and went. Now I had to be this trophy that Bishop could carry from church events to city events. I was exhausted most of the time. I hated having to smile for the camera and having to pose. It wouldn't be so bad if things were better at home. Then again, maybe this path could lead to better? Who knows?

New Salem had seen an increase in membership because of Bishop's new position as Councilman. With that came an increase in couples idolizing us and using us as the blueprint for their relationships. I went from feeling trapped to feeling completely entombed. If there was a chance that the desire to leave would spring up again, it was gone now. There were too many eyes on us to run the risk of such a scandal. The pseudo-celebrity status now followed us outside of the walls of New Salem. It was a smothering feeling and I was secretly begging God in my heart to set me free from the weight somehow.

Chapter 13

About the Children

I was a shell of the old Brooke. I felt so ashamed and stupid. If my life were a movie or a book, I'd be yelling at the main character to get out if she were in a situation like mine. I couldn't understand why I felt like I had to stay. I was living on shallow breaths. I had given Bishop my everything, and now here I was with nothing but mixed emotions to show for it.

His representative had left the building. I was nothing more than a wind-up doll for the man I actually married to bring out when he was playing the part of Man of God or Servant of the People. In private, he would throw the doll on the floor. Most of the time, his emotional and mental manipulation had me walking on eggshells for fear of setting him off and wondering, *What did I do so wrong, Lord?* I was swinging like a pendulum – stay to honor your commitment...leave to save yourself...stay and pray...leave and live.

My heart wanted to become a mother, and my soul wanted to make Daddy a grandfather. But my mind needed the escape hatch of no children. There were moments when it seemed like we could make our marriage work, but they were fleeting and getting to be farther and farther in between. I didn't have the energy to try anymore. I felt so invisible. Here I was sacrificing and slaving away to support Bishop and his ambitions. But, whenever it came to mine, I would have to approach him with specific requests and remind him repeatedly to get less than his best every single time. During lucid moments, I would beat myself up for not looking long enough or close enough to see the red flags. If Bishop were a case, I would refer him to another attorney. If only I could go back in time to stop myself from rushing into marriage.

In between our passive-aggressive fights, Bishop was trying to pressure me into giving him children for the fairytale. He wanted a boy and a girl in that order. Although we had talked about building a family together, I knew we weren't ready. Bishop was reckless with spending. I didn't want my children to want for anything. I had fears that if I started a college fund, he would raid it without me knowing until it was too late. I didn't want my children to see his drunken fits. I didn't want them feeling the pressure I felt to maintain the picture-perfect-public image.

At the time, I was wrestling with a voice that whispered, *Maybe motherhood will make him love you.* All I wanted was to feel loved and appreciated. I didn't love myself enough to leave. And, I wasn't sure if God was punishing me. Could I be in this living hell because I got so lost in what I thought I wanted that I made God jealous? Had I turned the idea of having a husband into an idol and not known it? There was never a day where I wasn't bombarded with questions. Then one day, Bishop did something that totally caught me off guard. He suggested that we go to New York City for my birthday weekend. I was so stressed out behind my workload that I wasn't even thinking about my birthday. I'm not going to lie, the fact that he remembered made me smile on the inside.

I was desperately trying to stave off how fast how our marriage was tanking, and now it seemed as though I was being given a ray of hope. I thought we could visit a jazz club and recreate our dating passion. There were some museums and other attractions in the city that I thought would help bring back the spark. In my heart, I wished that the weekend getaway Bishop initiated would make up for the disaster that was our honeymoon. I was excited for the first time in a while. The plan was for me to head into the city by train and meet Bishop at our hotel. He had an obligation at the church that he needed to take care of first and didn't want me to be forced to wait for him to finish. I was supposed to set the mood for the weekend by getting something sexy at my favorite lingerie boutique.

I clocked out early that day, stopping at the house to grab my things before Ubering to the train station. I made sure that Bishop's packed bags were waiting at the door so he wouldn't have to waste time. I journaled on the train ride. I wrote about the butterflies I had and the hope that we were going to be able to make things right after such a rocky start. I arrived an hour early before check-in. I dropped off my bags at the hotel so I could go shopping for that something sexy. On the way, I found the most gorgeous black dress I've ever seen. The glitter accent on the dress made it seem as though I was draped in the night sky itself. My shopping trip expanded to a hunt for matching shoes. I imagined that this was the perfect way to rekindle our flame. I wanted us to fall in love with one another all over again.

I got back to the hotel in good time to shower and get ready. The dress fit me like a glove. It made me feel absolutely regal. I couldn't wait for Bishop to see me. The reservations were set. I found a nice club that had the most perfect view of the New York City skyline. The only thing missing was Bishop. I texted him to see what his ETA was for the night. He messaged me saying that he was running late and to go on ahead to the restaurant so we wouldn't lose the reservation. I obliged. This restaurant filled pretty quickly and reservations usually had to be made weeks in advance. I found myself repeatedly turning down the advances of the taxi driver chauffeuring me to the restaurant. It was strange, even though I wasn't interested, the sudden attention made me laugh. It made me realize how affection starved I was in our marriage. I survived the drive through the hectic city traffic and the driver's attempts to guilt trip me into giving him my number. Sure enough, there was a long line waiting outside the restaurant. I entered in and checked in with the hostess. I was seated almost immediately, much to the disdain of the walk-ins waiting for a table. I sent Bishop another text, asking how much longer he was going to be. No response. I chalked it up to him probably wrapping up, driving, or being on the train. It was awkward each time my server asked me if I was ready to order. The server was small and almost mousy looking. Her glasses seemed to slide down her nose each time she lowered her head to take my order. My response never changed, "I'm waiting for my husband. He's on his way and I don't want to order without him." By the third time, she gave me a look that seemed to say, "Sure, Jan."

I called Bishop to see how much longer I was going to have to wait. The phone went straight to voicemail. I had been waiting for almost an hour. I became increasingly aware of how embarrassing the situation was becoming. Occasionally, I caught the stares of curious onlookers from the surrounding tables. I could feel the pity that came from the waitstaff. At one point, the manager brought over a bottle of wine and said that it was on the house. I could only imagine how pathetic I looked. I called Bishop five more times. Straight to voicemail. Every. Single. Call. I started to wonder the worst scenarios. *What if he got into an accident on the way here? What if someone tried robbing him as he left from the church?*

I reached out to Cathy, our church's worship leader. She was supposed to be there with Bishop during this meeting. She sounded flustered when I called her. It was like I caught her in the middle of something.

"I'm sorry, First Lady, I'm not sure where Bishop went. He said he was heading home after our meeting. Would you like me to call him and let him know to give you a call?" I gave her a very defeated no and told her it was fine. It wasn't.

I couldn't figure out what in the world was going on in Bishop's head. I sat frozen in shock, uncomfortable at the sudden awareness that I was alone on my birthday. After some time, the server came back and let me know that they were getting ready to shut down the kitchen and if I wanted to order something, they could make it to go. I don't remember what I said. I don't even remember if I got a bill. I wouldn't see Bishop again until I returned home early the next day. I was so upset I didn't even bother calling Bishop to tell him I was coming home. This was supposed to be our moment to reset and get everything right. When my Uber pulled up to the front of the house, I noticed something strange. Cathy's car was parked in my driveway. It wasn't often that she visited our house, at least I didn't think so. Alarm bells started going off in my head. I struggled to get my bags to the door without making a bunch of noise. I had to find out what was going on.

I carefully opened the door and hurried to get my bags inside in order to disarm the alarm before it went off. When I turned to disarm it, I saw that it had already been disarmed. I was puzzled and trying to ignore the sinking feeling in the pit of my stomach. My ears perked up to the sound of giggling coming from the living room, followed by Bishop's familiar bellow. I could feel the heat rising in my face. My ears were hot. I clenched my hands so hard that I thought my nails were going to draw blood. I left my bags at the door and hauled off toward the laughter. I will never forget what I saw; Bishop was curled up with Cathy on the couch watching as her two children played in *my* living room. Before I could ask what the hell was going on, I heard something that shattered my heart into a million pieces.

"Daddy, when are you coming back home?" the little girl asked. She couldn't have been more than six years old.

Her brother then echoed her sentiments, "Yeah, Daddy…"

I let out an audible gasp, startling Bishop and Cathy. "Oh my God, Brooke?! What are you doing *here*?"

I shook my head uncontrollably, "This is why you left me alone on my birthday? So you could entertain *your* family in *our* house? You were supposed to-,"

"Brooke, I can explain. Let's go talk in the kitchen-," He started to slowly rise from the couch with his hands forward like he was going to try to grab me.

I took a step back. "NO! YOU THINK YOU COULD JUST EXPLAIN SOMETHING LIKE THIS AWAY?! YOU'VE HAD A WHOLE 'NOTHER FAMILY BEHIND MY BACK?! WHY WOULD YOU DO THIS TO ME?! YOU SHOULD HAVE LEFT ME ALONE!"

Bishop turned back to look at Cathy. "Why don't you take the kids to the car? I'll meet you there."

I wanted to tear into Cathy, but when I saw the children that I had never seen before huddling together afraid, I shrunk inside myself.

"Stephan, Stephanie, come on babies, let's get your coats."

"Mommy, what is the scary lady going to do to Daddy?" Stephan asked.

Cathy didn't answer. She snatched Stephan's tiny hand as she picked up Stephanie. She didn't say anything to me. No apology. Nothing. She refused to look me in the face.

The room felt like it was spinning. I had to sit down. Bishop ran over to my side. I wasn't sure if he was feigning concern or if he was seriously worried about me.

"Brooke, I'm sorry. I was going to tell you, but I didn't know how. Talk to me, please…"

I was so broken in that moment. The most I could do was stare at the floor. Bishop stammered in an attempt to come up with some sort of excuse.

"Cathy and I used to be married when I was a chaplain in the Navy. But things didn't work out. I didn't want anything to do with her but she had my son. The little girl definitely isn't mine."

I didn't want to hear it. I was over it. I was hearing Sam Smith singing, "I Know I'm Not the Only One" in my head:

You and me we made a vow, for better or for worse. I can't believe you let me down, but the proof is in the way it hurts…

Someone else inside of me was speaking, "Bishop, that's bull and you know it. She looks just like you."

He turned away from me. I could see tears welling in his eyes. He wasn't crying because he hurt me. He was crying because he got caught.

"How come you don't love me, Bishop? Why did you even bother marrying me if this was how you were going to treat me?"

Bishop lowered his head and couldn't even look at me, "I do love you. I do…"

"No, you don't, Bishop. If you did, then you wouldn't do this to me. I know we said, 'for better or for worse,' but for worse is all that this marriage has been. What did I do to deserve this from you? You told me that I was your first and only wife. And now you were married before and in the Navy. It's like I married a stranger. It's like I wake up every day and find out a new reason as to why I don't know you at all."

"Babe I…"

"Don't Babe me, Bishop. I have given you everything. What more do you want from me?"

Bishop sat in silence for a few moments, "I want kids, Brooke. But it's like whenever I go to touch you, you're too busy. You're always working and you don't have time for me."

I was flabbergasted. "Are you serious right now?! You already have kids apparently, so I don't know why you're not satisfied. Even if you didn't have those children, what would change? Do you want to know why I'm always working, Bishop? It's because it seems like I'm the only one who's supporting us financially. I cover all the bills. I pay for all of the nonsense that pops in your head. I pay for all of your mistakes. Maybe I wouldn't be so tired if you actually pulled your weight.

"You think we're ready for kids with all of this mess going on? If I take time off from work behind our children, who's going to support us? Are you going to step up to the plate? Because if you have no plans for that, I see no reason bringing a child in this world. I don't want my babies to want for anything. You've put me through hell. You don't need to do that to them too. And how are you even supporting the kids you have now? Are there any more kids or wives that I should know about? Is this why you picked the job at this church? So you could be closer to your kids?"

Bishop began to bawl, placing his head in my lap. "I'm so sorry, Babe. I was weak and I didn't mean it. I just want to have a family with you. That's all I want.

I was stupid and I shouldn't have done that to you. Please forgive me."

"It's not that easy, Bishop…"

"Listen Brooke, I will do whatever it takes. All I ask is that we start working on building our family. Please."

"Did you even listen to anything I just said?"

"Brooke, you have to have faith, Brooke. God will

bless us. You'll see. Let me make this up to you. Forgive me. Please."

"Before I even consider giving you kids, you have to promise me that you will only see Cathy for the kids, and I have to be around. I don't trust you."

"It's a promise. I'll make it up to you. You'll see." I was suspicious on how quickly he said that. I couldn't put my finger on it. Something felt off. The promise felt empty. I was so torn down by everything. *Why didn't I cuss him out and end it right then and there?*

Chapter 14

Getting To Know All About You

Two Years Later

Marriage has turned my life upside down. What started out as a fairytale ended up being a little shop of horrors. Everything I knew was built on a lie. Ryan never mentioned that he was divorced when we first started dating. He never mentioned that he had kids. Each day, I felt as if the ground was shifting beneath me. The seismic shifts shattered the mirrors on the walls in the masquerade of our marriage. My image as a wife was fragmented and pieces of glass were falling to the floor with each new falsehood. If he would have told me about his divorce, I would have been fine with that. Heck, I would have even had a chance to check and see if he was over his ex. I don't know how I would have responded if he would have told me he had children. I'm not sure if I would have wanted to meet the children first or maybe take a step back. My heart broke for them. They were so innocent in this matter.

They didn't ask to be here and I felt that my time with Bishop ended up stealing time from them. We had to be discreet in our coparenting approach. We couldn't afford for members of our church to find out that their pastor had children by the church's worship leader before he married the First Lady. I found myself questioning what he saw in her. I went to the gym to keep myself fit. Cathy looked like she could think about a Twinkie and gain weight.

Bishop always seemed like he was revolted when I put on a little weight. I remember how repulsed he was when I was hospitalized after my miscarriage. "I didn't think your body was going to look so disgusting," he said coldly. Any other time, I would have told him to take his opinion and shove it. But I was vulnerable after losing the baby. I felt foolish expecting comfort from him, and rationalized that it was a difficult time for both of us. He said he wanted to have a baby with me so badly. I still wanted one myself to keep my promise to Daddy. But I wasn't sure if I wanted to have Bishop's baby. He still had two children from Cathy to take care of. I had to force him to spend time with them and set up visits so they could see him. I knew he only wanted children with me for publicity purposes.

I wanted to call Mommy so badly. I wanted to drive home to her and Daddy and cry in their arms. I felt so alone. I don't know how I was able to function. I felt like the Tin Man in the Wizard of Oz. I had lost the use of my heart. Except my theme song was not *Follow the Yellow Brick Road*. It was Sade's *Soldier of Love*. I had combat boots instead of ruby slippers. The loving home of my childhood wasn't a place I could go back to. My house was nothing like a home. So, I sang with Sade. *I'm at the borderline of my faith. I'm at the hinterland of my devotion. I'm in the front line of this battle of mine. Still waiting for love to come and turn it all around.*

It was Bishop's week with the kids. I climbed into the passenger side and waited for him to join me in the car. Stephan and Stephanie were excited for this visit. Stephan had just turned ten the week before. We weren't able to celebrate his birthday with him because Bishop was sick the day of the party. I offered that we could take him to Six Flags New England to make up for it. The children had never been. Cathy only made so much on her salary from the church and Bishop did very little to help her financially. They didn't really get to have many experiences like this. They weren't even my children, but I wanted to give them the world. They didn't ask for their parents. Stephan was a little apprehensive toward me because he was a little older. Stephanie on the other hand, took to me like I was her second mom. She loved having tea parties with me during their visits. As sweet as those moments were, they were another shock to my heart. Spending time with the children, especially Stephanie made me realize how much I wanted to have kids of my own. I wanted a little girl of my own. I imagined how the girls would play together and grow close. I thought about what would happen if I had a boy instead. Stephan was a great big brother when it came to Stephanie. I hoped in my heart that if I did eventually have children, Stephan and Stephanie would welcome them warmly.

We made sure the kids turned in early the night before the trip. When I peeked in the guest room where they slept, they both were wide awake and too excited to sleep. I decided it was time for an impromptu tea party and made two small cups of Sleepy Time tea. It worked like a charm. We piled into the car early the next morning. The drive would take almost two hours and it would be even longer if we hit afternoon traffic, especially in Massachusetts. We had to be proactive to beat the rush.

The kids were knocked out in the back seat as we drove up. Bishop was quiet most of the drive, occasionally asking if we needed to hit a rest stop along the way. Once in a while I'd glance up in the rearview mirror to check on the kids. Stephan had Cathy's features but Stephanie looked like Bishop could have spit her out. It still blew my mind that he tried to deny her when she looks so much like him. Looking at them reminded me of the hole I had in my heart. I thought this was going to be our reality. Bishop's deceptions robbed me of many of the experiences that I was looking forward to. Whenever I felt willing enough to try to have a child with Bishop, he wouldn't want to touch me. But he was quick to be all in my face when I wasn't in the mood. In the back of my mind, I was scared he may have still been sneaking around with Cathy or someone else behind my back. It was a nagging feeling that just wouldn't leave me alone.

As we pulled up to the park grounds, the kids seemed to wake up on cue. Stephan happily exclaimed that he wanted to ride on the rollercoaster that you could see from the parking lot. Stephanie on the other hand was fixated on looking for Mickey Mouse.

Bishop haphazardly popped her bubble, "Wrong park, honey. Mickey Mouse is at Disney. Six Flags has Bugs Bunny and the Looney Tunes."

From my peripheral, I looked up at the mirror again and watched as Stephanie's face began to twist into melt down mode. "Bishop," I whispered through gritted teeth, "Why would you say that before we entered the park?"

He caught the tone in my voice and began to open his mouth to rolled back his mistake, but it was too late. Stephanie started hollering, tears flowing from her face. "I WANT MICKEY MOUSE!"

I stepped in trying to calm her down, "Stephanie sweetie, remember we're here for your big brother's birthday. But maybe, if you're good, then we can go see Mickey Mouse at Disneyland in the future, okay? Let's have fun today. You don't want to make your brother sad, do you?"

Stephanie sniffled, "No, ma'am," hastily wiping the tears from her face.

I handed her a napkin before gesturing to Bishop to let her calm down before we headed into the park. Once there was peace, it was time to start our day of fun. Stephan wanted to ride all of the rides that he was not big enough for. Stephanie wanted funnel cake and every stuffed animal that she laid eyes on. I would catch Bishop looking at the butts of other women in the park. His arm must have been sore from me punching him each time that I caught him doing it. Despite what was happening between their father and I, the kids seemed to be having a great time. It was around 3:00 PM when our sunny day at the park turned into a downpour. Rain wasn't supposed to come until the following week. Of course, the weatherman has a habit of getting it wrong. But then again, how often do they get it right? It was a mad dash to the car, all of us soaked by the time we reached it. Before I got in the car, I went to the trunk and grabbed a blanket to help the kids keep warm. Bishop started the car and ran the heat on full blast. The children excitedly chattered in the back, indifferent to our present situation. Stephan kept on going on and on about how this was his best birthday ever.

The rain was relentless and getting heavier by the minute. Stephan pressed his little face against the glass of his window, puffing air and watching how it fogged up the window. Stephanie lamented about how she forgot her iPad at the house. She wanted to watch *Frozen* for what would have been the millionth time. Poor thing was bored out of her mind. It wasn't long before her brother joined her in the boredom brigade. He went from puffing air at the window to licking it. I decided to distract them with a game of *I Spy!* I wasn't sure how much we were going to be able to see. However, it seemed as though the odds were shifting in our favor. Although it was still raining, sunlight could be seen peeking from the clouds. I was hoping that meant the rain was going to let up soon.

"I spy with my little eye," I looked up and down the road. I scanned the car carefully. Finally, I found my target. "Somethinnnngggg...red."

Stephan and Stephanie looked around, bickering over what it could have been. Suddenly, something caught Stephan's eye. "Is it the little tree on the mirror?" He correctly picked the air freshener that was dangling on the mirror.

"Great job, sweetie. Okay, it's your turn." He happily snickered and got to work looking for his target. I could feel the car begin to slow down. Traffic was coming to a stop up ahead thanks to what looked like an accident. *Great, we're going to be here for a while.* I let my attention return back to the kids and our current game. I watched him focus on something that was outside of the car. It was a Navy billboard. I figured he may have gravitated toward that because of Bishop. I watched as he pretended as if he was still searching for something.

"Ahem, I spy with my little eye…something blue." There was a matter-of-fact tone in his voice as he crossed his arms over his side of the blanket.

Stephanie threw out her guesses as I threw out mine. I waited a bit before I revealed my real guess. "Is it that Navy billboard?"

Stephan sucked his teeth, "How'd you guess so fast?"

"Well, your daddy was in the Navy, right? It made my guess easy." I said with a laugh.

A confused look appeared on Stephanie's face. "Daddy was in the Navy?" She looked at her brother who returned her expression with a shoulder shrug. "But Daddy, I thought you worked for *Old Navy*?"

Stephan echoed his sister, "Yeah Dad, you weren't in the Navy. You worked at Old Navy for a long time. Wasn't that where you met Mom?"

Bishop did not break his stare from what was ahead. He must have felt me drilling holes in his head with my eyes. Nervously, he cleared his throat.

"What's that, Bishop? I don't think Stephan heard you agree that you met their mom at Old Navy and *she* was in the Navy?"

My words were pointed, yet restrained. I didn't want to let the kids know about the tension building in the car.

"Y-y-yeah. It was Old Navy…" He still refused to look at me. His grip tightened around the steering wheel.

"So, when did you become a chaplain? Or was that your cousin *Charlie Chaplin?*" I wanted him to look at me and lie again. But I wouldn't get that satisfaction. Bishop refused to say anything else. I turned my head toward the backseat. "Stephanie honey, why don't you take my turn since I went already?"

"Okay, Bibi. I spy…"

The sound in the car went to static. The man driving was an intimate stranger who used to work at Old Navy as an adult. *Why didn't I walk away when I saw the coupon on our first date?*

Chapter 15

Call Me Bishop

After we returned home from the Six Flags trip, I waited for the children to go to bed before I interrogated Bishop about his past. He begrudgingly admitted the story that he gave me when I found out that he and Cathy had children together was a lie. But what he told me next made me sick to my stomach.

"It was actually Cathy who was the Navy chaplain. When we met, it was because she stopped in the store to talk to a friend of hers that also worked there. We hit it off right away and things were a whirlwind. She ended up getting pregnant and we got married to avoid a scandal. She couldn't serve while visibly pregnant, that would have been a disgrace. She had written all of these sermons in advance. So, I convinced her to let me preach them.

"Cathy ended up getting pregnant again. By that time, our marriage was over. I thought that she had cheated on me. So, I left and I took her sermons with me. I've been preaching them over the years. I've written my own since then but...I still go back and revisit them from time to time. If Cathy would have chosen to go after me to get the sermons back, she would have been exposed and lost her position and the benefits. Instead, she put in a request to step down for the sake of being with her children as a single mother, and they gave her a release. I wasn't expecting to see her when we came to New Salem. I was scared she would bring the sermons up again, but exposing the truth would bring her down as well. Now that the children are getting older, I don't think she wants to run that risk. It's not like I have feelings for her or anything. She's the mother of my kids and that's it. I don't think she has any feelings for me either. It's just a kumbaya for the sake of the kids."

I couldn't believe the audacity of this man. He had this pattern of destroying the lives of the women that were attached to him. The way he said everything was so cold. It was like he couldn't see the wrong in what he did.

He hijacked Cathy's whole life. I could only imagine what it would have been like if he started to go around and tell people that he was a lawyer and began to take credit for my cases. My gut told me that Cathy has probably wanted to say something about this for a while. Children be damned, I would have. But I know how manipulative and conniving Bishop can be. Sadly, I'm also familiar with the lingering fear that's probably keeping Cathy quiet.

Two things were for sure. I had to get to the bottom of this, and I had to be discreet. This wasn't all that Bishop was hiding from me. I wasn't planning on being around when the rest hit the fan. I needed to gather up what I needed in order to finally break free once and for all. As the saying goes, "The enemy of my enemy is my friend." I had to talk to Cathy and we needed to be alone. The tables seemed to be turning in my favor. Bishop was in the process of preparing for this fancy schmancy anniversary gala to celebrate his tenure in ministry. Oh, the fraudulency! I was settled on my plan. Find Cathy. Find the truth.

I waited until Bishop went to a scheduled meeting with his campaign chair across town. Cathy was scheduled to be in the church office for worship planning. I was a little anxious driving to New Salem that day, but I needed to plan my exit. Cathy had avoided me for the most part once I found out about the children she had with Bishop. She only interacted with me when she had to help keep up Bishop's illusion. I began to sympathize with her in my heart. He made her out to be this villain that was threatening our existence, when in actuality, he was the real offender. He had Cathy in his grasp, and I was determined to not only set myself free, but to liberate her too. I pulled into the parking lot and sat in my car for a few minutes. I watched as various people carried decorations out of the church for the gala. The celebration wasn't supposed to go on for another week. But Mr. Big Stuff – that really should be his theme song… *Mr. Big Stuff, tell me. Who do you think you are, Mr. Big Stuff?* Anyway, Bishop, wanted to live it up as much as possible. I said a silent prayer and headed to the church office.

As I walked down the hallway, I could feel my heart beating out of my chest. I wasn't sure what Cathy was going to do or say, or if she would even react at all. I wondered how she must feel seeing me with Bishop after he abandoned her and their children. Did she still have feelings for him? Have they hooked up behind my back? Has he said anything to her about our relationship? I had so many questions. I got closer to the office and could see Cathy hunched over the desk and furiously scribbling on something. She was too focused to see me coming. I reached for the door handle and paused, letting my hand hover over it. The thought of aborting the mission crossed my mind. I pushed on the handle without even realizing it. *It's now or never, I guess.*

"Hi. How can I hel-," Cathy wasn't expecting me to be standing in the doorway. Her face went pale at the sight of me. She almost lost her bearings trying to get to her feet. "Lady Black, I'm sorry, I wasn't expecting you. Did you need-,"

I raised a hand in the air to stop her, "Please, Cathy. It's more than okay for you to call me Brooke by now. We're pretty much family at this point, thanks to Bishop." I could see Cathy trying to process that last statement. I gestured for her to take her seat once again and I sat in the chair in front of her desk. "There is something that I need your help with. I need to know the truth about Bishop once and for all. Is it true that he was never a Navy chaplain and the sermons that he has been preaching over the last few years have been yours?" Cathy's face cracked at my question, her tears breaking the dam of emotions that she held on to for so long. She echoed everything that Bishop said and then some.

"Stephanie had a problem with her heart when she was born and that was a huge financial burden. There was only so much I could do by myself. When I saw that

Bishop was coming to New Salem, I thought this was the chance for him to finally do right by his children, especially Stephanie. He promised that he would start doing more to take care of her, I just had to call off the child support order. I told him that I couldn't do that, not after he ghosted me for years. He then tried to say that he planned on divorcing you and we'd be a family again. Part of me wanted to believe him. But I know his tricks by now. Nothing he says is ever true... especially after I saw him with his ex-fiancée recently."

"HIS WHAT?!" In my head. I had to stay calm, cool, and collected so she would keep the information flowing freely. I felt myself treating this like discovery for work. Plus, the fact that Cathy just indirectly told me that she would go back to Bishop if the opportunity presented itself, let me know we weren't allies after all. I was stuck on the revelation that there was another woman on his totem pole and I needed to see where she ranked. What'd I miss while I was trying to process these last two tidbits? Her mouth was still moving.

"He was engaged to Kelly before we met. She comes from a real affluent family. Bishop's folks were nothing to sneeze at either, but he didn't have what was needed to maintain their level of greatness. So, he always had to use someone to get ahead. It was my understanding that she dumped him because he couldn't get his act together. Imagine my surprise to see him parading around with her a few days ago."

"Cathy, do I know Kelly?"

"I'm shocked you haven't met her yet because you've definitely seen her around Bishop. She's his campaign chair and the one who has been doing all the planning for this gala. And when I saw them together…it didn't look like they were discussing anything campaign related. He never really got over her. I always felt her shadow even when Bishop and I were together. It made me feel like I was never good enough. I can't believe I almost let him sucker me into an affair with him again."

As I was drowning in a tsunami of emotions, I flashed back to that initial dinner table with Bishop and his parents. I remembered how Ella kept bringing up his *friend*, Kelly, and now it made sense. She wanted to get prestige back into her family since her son hadn't measured up.

Mission accomplished here. I got Cathy's side of the story. I thanked her for her time and prepared to go. But, like Columbo, there was one thing I needed to know.

"Cathy," I paused, "why haven't you gone after Bishop for all he did to you? Are you afraid of him?"

She looked at me, her eyes sullen, "I wish I could say I was *afraid,* but fear doesn't even begin to cover what this man makes me feel. And I pray, Brooke, that you never have to find out."

I reached out for her hand and squeezed it. "And I pray, Cathy, that there comes a day when you are free from his spell."

Letting go of Cathy's hand, I began to take my exit. A delicate whisper followed me out, "Brooke…I'm sorry."

I was dazed on the drive home. The reality was that I was just another person on Bishop's growing laundry list of props. Were there others out there? Probably. Was it possible that he had more kids out there? I wouldn't put it past him. Bishop's car was the only one in the driveway when I got home. Part of me expected to see Kelly's Maserati waiting for me. I couldn't fathom how the other woman was beneath my nose the entire time. Or if Cathy was right about him not getting over Kelly, maybe that made me the other woman? I opened up the door to see Bishop dancing around in the kitchen and drinking a glass of white wine. Sebastian, now an old geezer of a pooch, looked on from the couch in what seemed like judgement. Seemed like my four-legged fur baby caught on that something was amiss, too.

I guess it's time for another scene in *The Good Wife* drama that has become my life… "You seem to be having a lot of fun, Bishop Black."

Taking another sip of his drink, Bishop flashed a cheesy grin as he swayed his hips. "Well, I was waiting for my dance partner to get home. I can't be having two left feet at this gala. We have to look our best."

I looked at Sebastian, "I guess that means you're fired, buddy." To which he replied, "Wuff!" I think that translates to "Shade!" in human speak.

Bishop placed his drink on the counter and sauntered over, taking my hand, and pulling me close to him. I rested my head on his chest. I could smell the cologne I loved so much with the scent of something I couldn't place. It must have been Kelly's perfume. He was with allegedly working on his campaign. I couldn't let him know that I knew about them. So, I did what any other woman would do; *fake it*. I faked it all through the week, I faked it in service. And I faked it the night of the gala.

Now that Cathy was no longer hiding from me, she played look out for when Little Miss Thang arrived to the extravaganza. All eyes were on her when she finally appeared wearing a bold, red dress with a plunging neckline. With the way her hair was styled I assumed she was trying to be Josephine Baker cosplaying Jessica Rabbit. I wanted to vomit. I noticed that she had come alone. After exchanging pleasantries with a few of the guests, she made her way over to where Bishop and I were seated. She greeted us the way I imagine the serpent greeted Adam and Eve in the garden, or the way Kaa greeted Mowgli in *The Jungle Book.* Adding insult to injury, she casually took the empty seat on the other side of Bishop. Everything about her was so fake. I wanted to leap across the table and snatch her wig off in front of everyone. But I wasn't going to let this man and his shenanigans embarrass me further. No, no, Brooke Rivers was about to make a comeback and she wasn't going to tolerate this foolishness anymore.

Kelly said something to me about my dress. I took the compliment and threw it over my shoulder with an invisible hand. *The nerve of this hussy.* Her perfume overpowered us at the table. Sure enough, it was the same scent that I had smelled on Bishop a few days before. A campaign staffer came over to the table and whispered something in Kelly's ear and she excused herself from the table. It was time for her to give a speech congratulating Bishop. It was longwinded and one giant stroke for his ego. I glanced over to Cathy at another table. Her eyes seemed to say, "I know. Me too, girl." A spotlight then blanketed the table, almost blinding me.

"Ladies and gentlemen, I'd like to welcome the man of the hour, Bishop Ryan Black, to the stage."

Bishop arose from the table with a soft chuckle. The grin on his face said that he believed he was going to have his cake and eat it too. He strode up to the stage. His demeanor said, "I'm a chauvinist pig and a narcissist, but I know how to hide that from everyone. Let me pretend that I am this beautiful, humble person so I can continue to soak everything out of everyone." He greeted Kelly with a kiss on the cheek when he got to the stage. He lingered for a bit, seeming to whisper something in her ear. She blushed and giggled. I wanted to throw my shoe at them. But I couldn't let him take me out of my element. And, by the way, there were too many white people at this event for me to act a fool.

Finally, Bishop approached the podium, "Thank you, Kelly for your kind words. But there's no need for everyone to be so formal with me. Please, just call me Bishop."

Chapter 16

Distractions

Dear Brooke,

As I am going to be out of the office for the next two weeks, I wanted to reach out to you regarding the partner position. I am not sure if you are still interested, but I believe that we need your chutzpah, your brilliance, and your ideas. You have been a tremendous asset to the firm, and you took my feedback with grace and perseverance. You have shown yourself to really be the MVP of our firm, and for that I am extremely proud. I would like for you to think about revisiting this opportunity and discussing it when I return. In the meantime, there is a CEU conference coming up and I would like for you to attend as a representative of our firm. I look forward to following up with you soon.

Regards,

L.C.

That email was just the affirmation I needed after dealing with the unfolding drama that is known as Bishop Black to some and Councilman Black to others. It had been a while since I had a chance to get out from under him and enjoy being me. Even though I was only going to New York City for a few days, it was far enough for me to breathe. I was no stranger to NYU. I had attended conferences there before and always seemed to meet someone new and interesting. I remember there was one year where I met a guy who said the only reason he became a lawyer was because his brother wanted to sue their home state for the right to marry a chicken. No, not a scared person. A. Literal. Chicken.

It was all because he had heard about some crazy goat marriage incident in Sudan. The man said his brother claimed he wasn't attracted to the chicken, but that the chicken seemed to understand him more than any woman ever had. He knew the case would be a longshot, but it would give him enough viral notoriety to attract rare cases. I asked him if his brother gave the chicken a name because I thought the whole story was a joke. To my surprise, he looked me dead in the eyes and said, "Why yes, her name is Henrietta."

I was hoping that maybe I would bump into him again or something else would happen that would give me a good, much-needed, guttural laugh. I was tired of living on shallow breaths with a heavy heart. Though there were still some good days with Bishop, and I did enjoy spending time with Stephan and Stephanie; I just needed to have something for me and only me. I deserved to be just as happy as the people around me. It seemed as though God was beginning to remember me in my misery. The door opened once again to the path of becoming partner. I still had a chance. Maybe, since this wife thing wasn't working out, I could rediscover my worth in the work world.

The CEU had the usual hustle and bustle conferences were known for. I happened to bump into the chicken attorney. As expected, the case was thrown out of court. Despite that, his crazy plan worked and he built his practice with even wackier cases. Workshop after workshop, I soaked everything in. I asked so many questions in practically all of the panels I attended that I felt like some of the other attorneys were a little sick of me. I didn't care.

It was halfway through the conference when I decided that I was just going to grab something to eat on campus instead of venturing out in the city. NYU was a great school, but their food options catered to a much younger crowd. After getting some chicken stir-fry and a Pepsi, I took a window seat that had a nice view of a fountain in the center courtyard of campus. My eyes fixated on a couple that sat at the fountain. *Oh, to be young and in love.* The innocent sight left a bad taste in my mouth.

I went to get up from the table, and as I reached for my tray, a hand placed itself in my view. I looked up to see a handsomely chiseled face staring back at me. His eyes were silver like that of a wolf's, offering a beautiful contrast to his copper skin. His wavy salt and pepper hair was in a slick coif with an undercut. The tan suit he wore must have been borrowed from Obama, with the exception that he was tieless. Instead, his shirt was slightly unbuttoned letting a little peek of chest hair show. I must have been staring a little too hard as he grabbed my attention by the gentle clearing of his throat.

"I'm sorry. I don't mean to disturb you, but I saw you were sitting over here alone and I was wondering if I could sit with you? I noticed you in a few of the workshops I attended and I wanted to pick your brain about some of the questions you asked." I went to answer his question but was distracted by the smell of his distinct fragrance: Tom Ford's Ombre Leather. Even though it was a unisex fragrance, the smell seemed to carry differently if it was a man or woman wearing it. I almost bought it once for Bishop. But after the novelty of our marriage began to wear off, he began to settle for the scents of Axe and Old Spice. It was nice to be around a man that could appreciate the finer things.

I began to sit back down, "Uh, sure? The more the merrier, right?"

"Cool. Let me grab my food and then I'll join you. My name is David, by the way. And you are?"

"B-Brooke." He made me forget my name for a second.

"Brooke...I like that. I'll be right back" He flashed a smile, and chile...I had to wonder if Jesus was his dentist. I could feel that familiar pitter-patter in my heart. He came back to the table with what looked like the Mongolian Beef and a hearty kale salad.

Oh my God. He eats vegetables. Wait Brooke, what are you doing? The bar is in Hell. I know you've gotten used to Bishop doing the bare minimum, but raise the bar, Sis. Raise. The. Bar. I noticed that he placed a black metal card next to his tray. "Isn't it a little careless to just leave your credit card out in the open like that?" *See? He's messing up already.*

He let out a surprised chuckle, "You're right! I should be more careful. But this isn't a credit card."

I raised a brow, "It's not?"

"Nope, it's for my Tesla."

I almost spit out my drink, "A *Tesla*?!" *Wait a minute girl, I take that back. He got a Tesla. I'm sure we can find a divorce lawyer at this conference; you can get that paperwork started tuh-day!*

He let out another laugh, "Yeah, I tend to get that response a lot. The Model S comes with the option of a key card instead of a key fob. I usually keep it in my chest pocket. Heaven forbid I kept it in my wallet and lost both the card and my wallet."

I nodded wordlessly, trying to catch myself from looking like I was smitten. When he said that he was going to pick my brain, he meant it. He asked me what I thought about policies, my firm, how long I had been in the field, stuff like that. I made sure that each time I answered one of his questions, I returned it with one of my own for him. He was originally from Santo Domingo, but moved to Brooklyn with his family at the age of 12. Hence why his *New Yawk* accent had a bit of a Spanish accent. Aside from working at a local firm that specialized in the stock market, he spent the majority of his time helping at a center for disadvantaged youth. He grew up poor and worked to take care of the parents that gave up everything to take care of him.

"I love kids. I've always wanted them, but I could never find the right woman to settle down with. I still have hope that it may happen one day. Otherwise, my Abuela will turn over in her grave if she doesn't get a great grandchild. I was my parents' miracle baby. There's a lot riding on me, I guess. Do you like kids, Brooke?"

The deeply personal question stabbed at my heart. "I'm married, with two step-children, but none of my own. Not yet anyway." I lowered my eyes and twiddled my ring.

"Forgive me for asking," David paused and appeared to contemplate if he really wanted to ask the next question. "I apologize if this is personal, so please don't feel like you have to answer. I saw that you were married, but when you brought it up just now, you didn't sound too happy."

I fumbled to find the words to respond, but no sound would come out. He saw right through me. I didn't want to act in desperation. I was wary because the last time I felt this way was when Bishop was lying to me about who he was and how he felt about me. It may have been the lightness of his eyes, but David seemed to peer deep into my soul. I felt that I could trust him. Yet, I was scared.

He reached out for my hand and held it. He didn't say anything, he just held it in silence. Such a reassuring touch reminded me how starved I was of simple affection. I could feel the tears beginning to well up. I forced myself to keep it together because this was the last place that I wanted to break down. David gave my hand a squeeze, "I know how you feel. I was married once. She was someone I really loved. We just - we couldn't see eye to eye on the things we used to. There were things about her that seemed to contradict the person I fell in love with. She wasn't a bad person, she just ended up being bad for me. Eventually, it felt better to part ways than for me to keep playing Russian Roulette with my heart. I'm not sure if you're in a similar situation, but I think I just might understand your hurt."

I mouthed the words, "Thank you."

David gave me a knowing nod. "If you need a friend to talk to, I'm here for you."

David and I ended up spending the remainder of the conference together. I found safe space in his comfort. When we weren't busy with conference related things, we travelled around the city. David was very chivalrous. Every door was held open, including the car door. He made sure I was seated first. If we walked on the sidewalk, he always walked on the side that was next to the street. He paid for all the meals we ate and refused my offers to cover the tip. I noticed that our servers would always wear a silent look of shock on their face whenever he handed them his card. When I saw it, it looked like just a plain, silver credit card. I nosily prodded as to what kind of card it was because I honestly had never seen it before. His answer revealed the reason why, "Oh this? This is the J.P. Morgan Reserve Card. It's sent by invitation only." I could tell that he was trying really hard not to sound like he was bragging. He may have even been a little embarrassed. I waited for him to go to the bathroom before I pulled out my phone to look up more details on the card. *Invitation only…must have excellent credit…at least ten MILLION IN ASSETS?! LORD, WHAT?! Jesus, what an upgrade!*

David was not a forceful man. He was careful not to make me feel as though I was being cornered into accepting something given that I was still married. There was something sexy about the restraint he had. In the beginning, I only wanted to get back at Bishop, but the more I got to know David, the more I realized I wanted this. I wanted him. On my last night in the city, I visited David's penthouse suite. He gave me a duplicate key so I could let myself inside. I nervously turned the key to see rose petals were scattered about. A bottle of Domaine Leroy was chilling on the table accompanied by two empty wine flutes. The lights were tastefully dimmed. I announced aloud that I arrived. David stepped into the room, wearing a burgundy suit, in his signature tieless fashion. He pulled a chair for me to sit at the table. Just then, the bell rang. He had a meal specially catered for our last night together. It felt like I was in a dream. When I thought he didn't have any more up his sleeve, he went back in the bedroom and came back out with a black guitar. He serenaded me in Spanish, sweeping me even higher off my feet. Even though I couldn't catch all of the words, the melody was clearly *Think About You* by

Luther Vandross. My heart heard, *So close to paradise, but closer than I should be. It's like I'm along for the ride, it happened unexpectedly.*

Then, I heard the clock chime, "It's getting late, maybe I should go…" I feigned like was going to grab my things.

"I would rather you stay, Brooke. But I'll respect whatever decision you make." His twinkling, starlit eyes echoed his wish for me to stay.

"Well…since you put it that way…I guess I could stay a little longer." I slid next to him, letting his strong but tender touch lift my head to face him. David leaned in, kissing me until I was breathless. The traces of him lit me on fire. I hadn't felt like that in so long. Suddenly, I stopped him.

"Brooke? Are you okay? Do you want me to stop?" I was oddly comforted by the worry in his voice.

"David…if we do this…promise me that you won't break my heart…"

"Brooke, if I ever break your heart, I'll give you mine in its place."

Hungrily, I searched for David's kisses again, letting the fires of passion consume us both until sunrise.

Chapter 17

The Last Chance

Meanwhile, back at New Salem, trembling hands and sweaty palms were gripping tightly to a phone. *Ring! Ring! Ring!* A voice on the other end answered, "Marshall & Marshall. How may I direct your call?"

Hands gripped tighter to the phone. Sweat beaded on the brow and slowly slid down the summit of the caller's face. "Yes…hi…I'd like to speak to an attorney. It's about Councilman Black…"

Three months had passed since I met David at the CEU. My body hummed a melody that I hadn't felt in a long time, and Bishop was none the wiser. David and I still texted from time to time. He understood that my situation was complicated, and let me know that his door was open for me if I wanted or needed him. I was starting to feel like my old self again. Partner was back in my sights. L.C. would drop hints that the position would likely be mine this time around. Mike was still trying to stir stuff up in the office until I pulled the, "When I say H, you say R," card. The CEU was only a short experience, but I came back with so much clarity. I was reminded of what I wanted to do, why I wanted to do it, and that I was dang good at it. I almost let Bishop and his mess take that away from me. After some deep soul searching and seeking after God, I began to focus in on the changes I wanted to see. God had moved for me before, and I anticipated that God would do it again. This time around, I wasn't going to try to help God help me. I was just going to let God do what God does best.

Getting in God's way was what left me vulnerable when it came to Bishop. God was trying to give me subtle warning signs that Bishop wasn't right for me, but I didn't listen. In a way, I felt a little like Sarah. Instead of trusting God's timing in sending my Isaac, I jumped the gun and was left with a wild donkey of a marriage in the spirit of Ishmael. What gave me hope was that God redeemed Sarah, and I knew if I just kept focusing on the work of my hands, that God would redeem me too. I couldn't believe that I had become so depressed that I honestly thought that God might leave me in the mess I made on my own. But as the Word says, *For I know the plans that I have for you. Plans to prosper you and not to harm you, plans to give you a hope and a future.*

I realized that I had done more than just make Bishop into an idol. I had also made an idol out of marriage. While there were external pressures, like fear of Daddy's condition, the occasional spam of wedding photos on my Facebook wall, and church folks that didn't know how to mind their business, I was responsible for the choices I made. But I wasn't going to fall for the lie that things had to stay this way forever. I decided since there was no healthy reason to fight for my marriage, I was at least going to fight for me. I resolved, *When I get home from work today, I'm going to tell Bishop how I feel. I'm not taking this anymore. I won't take this anymore. I'm choosing me this time. I don't care if that makes me selfish.* I sought to be in holy matrimony, I wasn't going to go another day settling for holey misogyny. I wanted my life back. I knew in my heart that Mommy and Daddy would be disappointed that I wasted so much time on this joker. But I also knew that they would be a lot happier that I finally came to my senses.

Bishop wasn't home when I pulled up in the driveway. I decided that I was really going to play this moment up. I ran a nice, hot bath, grabbed my favorite coffee scrub exfoliant, set aside a gold and collagen face mask, lit some candles, and poured a glass of my favorite wine. I enjoyed my DIY spa experience. I laid out my sexiest black dress, fixed my hair, and beat my face for the gods. My lasers were set to stun. I texted Bishop to pick up some Italian for dinner because I was too busy making his favorite cake to start on dinner. Bishop loved Black Forest cake, and I was going to bake him one that he would never forget.

When the cake was done, I piped some vanilla frosting on top to spell a special message. I could see Bishop's headlights creep up the driveway. I dimmed the lights, poured some more wine, and placed the cake in its position. I took my seat at the head of the table. I wanted Bishop to see me as soon as he walked in the door. Boy did he see me. He almost dropped the food in the process. *Yup, I know I look good. Too bad you're busy running around behind what's her name.* After Bishop came to his senses, he placed the food on the counter and quickly ran to my side of the table to place a quick peck on my forehead.

He looked at me hungrily, "So…what's the special occasion?"

"I have something special to celebrate!" I said before taking a slow sip of my drink.

"Oh?" his interest was piqued. As if on cue he sat in his chair. I knew he was waiting for me to be the beautiful subservient wife of his dreams. "Am I allowed to know?"

I decided to humor him. Taking the lobster alfredo, I glided over and placed a huge helping in his plate as seductively as I could before serving myself. "You'll find out before the night is over." Bishop looked at me with a raised brow. I made idle chit chat, letting him feel really good and full; full of drink and full of food.

Finally, he said the magic words that I was dying to hear all night. "So, where's my cake?" He let out a low chuckle and tilted his head, indicating he wasn't only thinking about the cake I baked.

"You want this cake, Bishop?" I said with the sweetest smile. He laughed some more, rubbing his hands together in anticipation. I placed the cake in front of him, keeping my hands on the lid so not to spoil the surprise.

"Oh, I want it. I mean it's mine, right?" The statement made me twitch. It stopped being "his" on our honeymoon.

"Haha...oh it's yours alright. I hope you like it. Now, come get it." I lifted the lid and watched his face go from gleeful to grim. There it was written on the cake in big, bold letters:

"IT'S OVER. I WANT A DIVORCE. 😊"

To add more salt to the wound, I took a cake knife and plunged it into the center of the cake. "Bon Appetit…" I then turned on my heel and went upstairs, leaving Bishop in the reality that he lost me.

I awoke the next morning to the smell of something almost nauseatingly sweet. Groggily, I opened my eyes to find that the whole bedroom was full of flowers. The bouquets seemed to go from the ceiling to the floor. It was hard trying to get to the bathroom because they almost completely blocked my path. Getting downstairs was another story. More flowers awaited me along with balloons that spelled out, "I'm sorry." This was giving me Buddy Love's half apology in *The Nutty Professor* vibes. A bouquet in the center of the kitchen table caught my attention. In it was a card with a handwritten apology promising that he would change if we could just go to counseling. Supposedly, Bishop didn't want to lose me or what we had. *Funny, that didn't seem to matter when it came to Kelly and Cathy.*

I decided to call Anita to pick her brain. If I was going to get a counselor, I may as well pick someone that I was familiar with. However, she advised that it would be best to pick someone who was neutral to the both of us. She was already my counselor, so her position was compromised. She didn't let me leave the conversation empty handed though. She gave me contact info for a few of her colleagues. I did my homework and searched among the options she provided before finally settling on Dr. August Bloom. When making the appointment I couldn't help but think he sounded pretty young to be a counselor. When we met, his voice didn't match his appearance. Steve Harvey had a doppelgänger from the 80s that was running loose, box cut and all.

I really didn't want to go through these sessions with Bishop. I didn't see the point. Bishop couldn't see that he couldn't have his cake and eat it too. He was still trying to be sneaky and play Kelly, Cathy, and me. He admitted that he still was trying to keep Cathy in his good graces. But he played dumb with me when it came to Kelly. Bishop asked if I ever slept around on him, citing his suspicions from when I came home from the CEU. Bishop had his secrets; I was going to keep mine. I bluffed. I think I said something along the lines that I was too busy trying to make partner this time to even think about fooling around. He fell for that.

I was fairly confident that David would be able to handle heat from Bishop, but I didn't want to send unnecessary trouble his way. The sessions were going nowhere. I didn't want to entertain the thought of taking Bishop back. If I didn't have so much going for me at the firm, I would have gone right to my parents' house. Of course, Bishop had a nasty competitive streak that didn't like losing. He decided to change up his tactics when he saw I was refusing to budge.

"I just want to be a better husband for Brooke. I know it was wrong of me to hide my kids instead of telling her. But I didn't want to take the special feeling away from her when we would eventually have kids. Her dad is sick, you know? I just wanted him to enjoy being a grandfather before his condition worsened."

Bishop kept his eyes to the floor. He knew in his heart that was a low blow. Daddy's condition hadn't worsened, but it wasn't improving. One of the things that I hate about Bishop is that he is a master manipulator who knows how to get under my skin.

"If I were a dying man, I would want to see my grandchildren while I still had the wherewithal to do so."

Just like that, he was back in my head, and I was beginning to reconsider everything.

Dr. Bloom suggested that maybe we should take a vacation where we could reconnect and get to know each other all over again. His rationale was that since the first honeymoon was not an enjoyable experience for me, a second honeymoon was an opportunity to enjoy something new. *Maybe things would get better with a do over?*

Bishop dropped hints that he would like to go to Aruba. Before I knew it, he went and booked two tickets for a round trip to Aruba and a stay at the most popular resort hotel. I didn't know what to expect on the plane. Part of me wanted to get excited. Still, there was a lingering feeling in the back of my mind to expect another shoe to drop. The first couple days seemed to go well. There was a day where we went shopping around the island. It was strange because it felt almost like we were the old us again. Bishop had seen a shirt in the window of a store and almost jerked my arm out of the socket running to look at it. It was a nice shirt that most tourists would come away with. One of those dressy island types. I encouraged him to try it on and it looked good on him. He happily went to purchase it…only for his card to decline. Embarrassed, he said, "Maybe that's a sign that I shouldn't get it." He looked really disappointed and since he probably spent most of his money on this second honeymoon experience, I felt it would make a good peace offering. As he walked out of the store, I shouted that I would lag behind for a moment because I saw something I wanted, and I bought the shirt as soon as his back was turned.

Relaxing in our suite under the air conditioning was something I was looking forward to after a long day in the sun. Bishop reclined in a chair on the patio. As he seemingly dozed off, I placed the bag with the shirt inside on his lap. The light pressure of the bag caused him to stir. He started to wake up a bit, confused by the bag. When he peeked inside, he was elated to see the shirt. "Brooke, you didn't have to do this." It was nice seeing the smile that made me fall in love with him so long ago. Then he took me way back to the days when he used to serenade me singing *Before I Let Go* by Frankie Beverly and Maze.

> *Now we've had our good times. That's what they say. We've hurtin' each other. Girl, it's a shame. I won't be foolish, no, no. I want to know. I want to make sure I'm right, girl, before I let go.*

This was Ryan – the man I fell in love with so long ago. But I had to steel myself and not fall for the charade. When he saw that I wasn't melting, his face went from happy to sad. "I'm sorry, Brooke. For everything... maybe we should pray about this...or maybe we should let things come to an end..."

What? You were just singing about us staying together. My head was spinning, and my heart was hurt when he brought divorce up again.

"But...if you're willing to try...I still am, too."

It seemed like he hesitated at the last part, and once again, I found myself at a crossroads. "Bishop...a moment ago you were singing about wanting us to work and proposing that we pray. Then you say our marriage should end. What's the point in trying when you're a double-minded man?"

"Brooke," his voice sounded like it was about to crack. "I really don't deserve you. I messed up so bad. But if God will help me, and you're willing, maybe we can turn this thing around?"

It felt like I was on a not-so-merry-go-round. How in the world could I be entertaining the idea of remaining in *this* relationship? As dazed and confused as I was feeling, somehow, I knew this wasn't quite the shoe that was going to drop and throw us both for a loop. Something much bigger was coming, but I wasn't sure what it would be.

Chapter 18

She's Wearing His Shirt

Bishop kept up his wishy-washy act for the remainder of our vacation. One minute he wanted to work things out, and then call it quits the next. Eventually, I was able to pull myself out of my feelings, choosing to play dumb the remainder of the trip. I reached out to my girls to try and vent. I was tired of keeping this to myself and I didn't want to give Cathy the opportunity to stab me in the back. Yvette wasn't returning my texts and Tina was sending me walls of texts about how I should fight for my marriage. I couldn't get a word in edgewise.

As soon as I would tap my screen to respond, in came another slew of messages. "Think about your image!" "Girl, men aren't perfect, do you really want to go back to being single?!" "Maybe there's something you could do for him in bed?" "Bishop is a good man, Brooke. Give him another chance." I couldn't believe how one of my best friends was taking his side over mine. The way she was talking, you'd think that maybe she had her eyes on Bishop, too. I gave up, putting my conversation with her on mute.

I thought about reaching out to David, but I knew the minute I'd hear his voice I'd wish he was with me instead of Bishop. And, that would only make things worse. *Guess I just have to be a big girl and suck it up.*

I let my thoughts drift toward the firm and started planning for my future. I didn't want to be teased with the promotion like I was the last time. Without being distracted by Bishop, I could dive right into my work. But sobering thoughts surrounding the state of my marriage were occupying my mind. Why was I so ready to believe that Bishop could change? In spite of everything, I was still hoping for Ryan's return. I remembered the days when his love flowed so freely through my veins giving me life. Now it was killing me softly, slowly poisoning the passion that we once had.

A lifetime ago I was convinced that the two of us could have taken on the world together – as true partners reaching for the stars together. Maybe Ella was shady toward me at our first meeting because she didn't see me as trophy socialite material like Kelly. But I'm always aiming for higher. It's not a goal if it's not beyond my reach. The sky may have been the limit for some, but I was willing to reach as far up and out into the depths of the universe as necessary to accomplish my goals, my dreams, my plans. My goals… my dreams…my plans were the only things I had left to give me comfort other than God. At one point I had almost thrown them away behind Bishop. I dedicated so much to give him the platform he wanted. But who was he? Nothing more than a scammer really. It was different when I thought we were doing something meaningful together. Changing lives. But he wasn't called to make disciples. He was working at Old Navy when he decided to steal sermons from Cathy. He had no problem stealing money from me. And, he was peddling Kelly's influence in politics. Our marriage was nothing more than a house of cards. I couldn't tell if it was crashing and burning because Bishop, as the big, bad wolf, was huffing and puffing and blowing it down or because the fire of his rage had extinguished our bond in the beginning. Either way, all that was left was ashes and embers.

The flight back was uneventful. Bishop sat next to me as if I was a stranger, occasionally making eyes at one of the flight attendants. I pinned my focus to the scenery outside my window. Aruba slowly shrank away from my view, seemingly being swallowed by endless blue. It was only a matter of time before we'd be back home. At least I was going to be able to give Sebastian a good cuddle. My eyelids became heavy as a gloomy tune filled my ears. *Somethin' happened along the way. What used to be happy was sad. Somethin' happened along the way, and yesterday was all we had...* I thought to myself, "After the Love is Gone," *hmmm. Fitting.* I gave into the pressure of sleep pushing down on my eyes. I fell asleep dreaming of that night with David. It was a cruel illusion, because for a moment, I thought I could smell his cologne.

In the weeks that followed, I found myself in meeting after meeting. Some for my promotion at the firm, others for church. Ironically enough, the only meetings that I was told I didn't have to attend were Bishop's campaign meetings. I wonder why *that* was? My pettiness began to bubble up again. I began to think about what would happen if I suddenly announced that we were divorcing at his next press conference and revealed his affairs in front of the world. It was a delicious thought, albeit for a brief moment. Scripture says, "we reap what we sow." I've had enough fruitless harvests behind Bishop. I don't need to open the door to more of them. I only had a little while longer to play the role of *The Good Wife*.

Once I made partner, I could sneak away and end things quietly. I'd give myself time to heal, and then… *maybe I could invite David for coffee?* It was funny how I found myself adding more guitar filled songs to my playlists and imagined him playing them for me. Still, part of me wondered if I was having one of those 'grass is greener' moments. Bishop's antics really did a number on my trust. I settled on crossing that bridge if I ever even got there.

Another Wednesday, another midweek Bible study. It was my turn to lead the ladies. Teaching was not my strong suit. I always preferred coming and listening. I wasn't a weak facilitator. I just wasn't interested in doing it. But you know, *the image.* I stared at the faces that I had grown accustomed to seeing week after week. Faces with wisdom etched into their cheeks. Youthful faces that still had the light of hope in their eyes. Then there were those who fell in between. I caught myself wondering what would happen to my relationships with these women once I left. It made me sad. Felt like a custody battle of sorts. The congregation was completely unaware of what was happening when they weren't around Bishop and me; completely innocent in the matter and most likely would remain stuck with him when I was gone. It was a nauseating reality.

There was something unusual in the air. Perhaps it was because I had a message that I actually wanted to share? Or perhaps because I was speaking to the single ladies? Whatever it was, I welcomed it. I opened my Bible to Matthew 10:13-14 and began to read:

> *If the home is deserving, let your peace rest on it; if it is not, let your peace return to you. If anyone will not welcome you or listen to your words, leave that home or town and shake the dust off your feet.*

"As women, we're expected to take and do a lot. As Miss Ella sang in *Madea Goes to Jail*, *'We gotta cook and clean and wash everything.'* But God did not create us to be indentured servants to our husbands. I've observed that many women are in this position. Instead of being patient and waiting for God's best, there's pressure to find a warm body and settle down. God really doesn't like us settling, let alone settling down. No, God wants us to settle *up*. So, what does this have to do with what Jesus says in this passage? I'm glad you asked. Your peace is the biggest indicator that you are in a place where God wants you. Bear in mind, I said your peace. Not a peaceful environment. Not the *piece* that you have tucked in your nightstand drawer. The peace I'm talking about is the one that comes from the Holy Spirit. It is a peace that sustains you when the going gets tough and the tough get going. It is the first thing that speaks to your discernment when red flags begin to appear. Your peace is powerful and far too often we ignore our peace to please other people. When it comes to our peace, we have to be on the lookout for things that rob us of it. For some, it may be your job. Others, it may be your spouse or your friends. This is not to be confused with minor frustrations or the periods where God is growing you. This is for when that nagging in your spirit gets louder and louder, and you tell it to be quiet because you don't want others to notice your discomfort."

Cathy was nowhere to be found when the women in the sanctuary broke into small groups to discuss the message of the evening. Usually, she was there to help out.

I had this weird feeling in the pit of my stomach. It seemed like an amplified version of what I felt prior to leaving for Aruba. As I mulled over my thoughts, the doors of the sanctuary suddenly flung open. The abrupt interruption startled us. Armed officers stared us down, guns drawn. We were terrified. Some of the ladies looked like they were getting ready to run. Fighting the tears welling in my eyes, I encouraged everyone to stay calm and not to make any sudden moves, even though the police had a history of making us targets whether we moved or not.

"What's going on? Are we in danger?!" I asked.

One officer gestured for the others to lower their weapons after they realized we weren't a threat. He then turned back to me, "We're looking for Ryan Black. We have a warrant for his arrest."

The room became so quiet that you could hear a butterfly land. Slowly the murmurs and whispers started. "Ryan?!" "Are they talking about Bishop?" "What could he have possibly done?" "He has to be innocent, right?"

Fire became caught in my throat. "Ryan? On what charges?"

"Failure to pay child support, ma'am," the officer replied.

Searing tears crashed against the shore of my cheeks. "I honestly don't know where he is. But if he's here, he'd be in his office." I pointed toward the stairs for the officers to go down to check. The room fell back to silence for a solid two minutes before we heard a commotion coming from Bishop's office. I could hear him yelling at the officers, followed by the sounds of a woman's voice. I nearly broke my neck trying to get to the hallway, the ladies following behind. I wondered if Cathy was actually with Bishop the whole time. Imagine my shock as I saw her walking in the doors of the church. *If she's just getting here…who's scream did I hear?*

I soon laid eyes on the answer to my question. The officers brought Bishop out, handcuffed in dress slacks, sock feet and an undershirt. As he was being carted away half-dressed and read his rights, a trembling Kelly emerged from his office wearing nothing but the shirt I bought him in Aruba. She was unashamedly screaming behind my husband as if he were hers. The witch was bawling her eyes out. Bishop couldn't even look me in the face as the officers pulled him past me. Kelly ran after him as they escorted him out of the church. I didn't feel embarrassed for me, and I didn't feel sorry for him. I felt numb all over. The other shoe had dropped. I was free now. My leaving wouldn't cause a scandal. He did that well enough on his own.

I looked over at Cathy, wondering what she thought of all of this. She looked up at me. Her eyes misty, but clear. She gave me a brief, knowing nod before whispering, "The spell is broken, Brooke. I'm free now. I'm free."

Chapter 19

Filing the Papers

The next morning, you'd think I'd wake up feeling good now that I was free as a bird, but I was…off. *Did last night really happen or was it all a dream?* I looked over at the other side of the bed and Bishop wasn't there. I threw the covers off myself and swung my feet over the side of the bed and just sat there for a moment to think. I closed my eyes, and I was taken back to the night before. I saw the women in Bible study. I remembered the conviction I felt as I delivered my exegesis of Matthew 10:13-14. I recalled the feeling of my heart about to beat out of my chest when the cops burst through the doors, guns drawn. I remember the sight of Bishop being led away in his underwear and being chased by that ho, Kelly, who was clad in the shirt that I bought him in Aruba.

I scoffed to myself at the irony of the situation. I never imagined that it would go down like this. This man, who made so much of an effort to put on airs of kindness, compassion, love, and humility to take on titles and positions he was in no way worthy of was led out of the church in front of his congregation in handcuffs in nothing but his underwear. To me, as messed up as this spectacle was, it was funny. It wasn't funny in a *haha* manner, but the fact that he was led out half-dressed was a portrait of how half-assed he had been ever since our horrifying honeymoon.

I looked up at the ceiling and marveled at the fact that last night actually happened. I was there, it was real, and in fact was neither a dream, nor a figment of my imagination. This revelation was confirmed by the amount of voicemails on my phone and my inbox blowing up with messages from the press reaching out to me for comment on the situation. Cathy's words immediately came back to mind as I sat with this realization and the memories of last night: "The spell is broken, Brooke. I'm free." Yeah, she was free all right, but me? I had some work to do and some loose ends to tie up before I could *really* be free.

In the days that followed, I grew much acquainted with the words, *no comment*. With Bishop out of the spotlight, it was shining ever-so-brightly on me and everyone wanted answers. I'd ignored most of the phone calls I received from the media. Heck, I even blocked their numbers only for them to use different ones. I'd responded to every email inquiry with a polite, "I have no comment" and left it at that. Short, sweet, and to the point, but I was wise enough to know that wouldn't be the end of it. Everywhere I went, be it work, my favorite coffee shop, or the grocery store, someone from the local paper, a blog, or the news was hounding me for information concerning the arrest, the charges, the mistress, the church, the city council, and the state of our marriage. It got so bad that I didn't want to leave my house, but Sunday was coming and what would it look like if Lady Black didn't show up for that? Especially after what had happened on Wednesday night. *Why did I ever agree to be a pastor's wife?*

There were days when I loved this role and other days where I dreaded it. Sunday was a day of dread. When my alarm went off, I hit the snooze button and tried to cling to what little sleep I got from the night before. The alarm sounded five minutes later, and I hit the snooze button again. This time, I stayed awake only to stare at the ceiling and go back and forth with myself over whether I would go to service or not. Sure, it was expected of me, but did I really have to deliver? They would understand why I wouldn't show up, but somehow, I had convinced myself that they were expecting me not to show up. I wasn't about to give them that satisfaction. They needed to know that this wasn't going to keep me from worship. I might have been married to Bishop, but my heart belonged to God. God was The One who strengthened me to withstand Bishop and to maintain decorum as First Lady. Just as I'd made my decision, the alarm sounded again. I silenced it, got up, and got myself ready.

I had showered, dressed, primped, and primed in record time. I'd decided on a more modest ensemble with a neutral makeup palette and a fitted navy-blue suit with simple diamond stud earrings and a matching single diamond necklace. I looked myself over in the mirror once my transformation was complete. After checking my teeth for lipstick, I was good to go. I grabbed my things and headed out the door, saying bye to Sebastian on my way out. As soon as I got outside, who else do I see but the press, still clamoring for a comment. I simply said, "No comment," and kept it moving. Last thing I needed was to be late on the one Sunday I actually needed to be in service on time.

I pulled into the parking lot just as Tasha Cobb's *Your Spirit* ended. I cut the engine and sat there staring at the church as I lightly gripped the steering wheel. Part of me wanted to run away so badly, but I knew I couldn't. I didn't know if it was my pride, my sense of duty, or even God telling me so, but somehow, I felt that I needed to do this. If I wasn't going to do it for me, I at least had to try for the sake of the congregation. So, I said a silent prayer, gathered my things, hopped out of the car, and made my way inside with my head held high.

As soon as I entered the sanctuary, a hush fell over the congregation. The music was still playing in the background, but if there was any conversation, it came to a halt as I was greeted by the shocked, awestruck gazes and a few open mouths of the members. *So, ya'll really weren't expecting me to show up, huh?* Well, here I am, and here I will be until everything is in place for me to make my exit. "Good morning, church," I said with a smile, once again assuming the role of *The Good Wife*. I got a few sheepish "good mornings" in reply. "Don't stop praising Him on my account. This is the day that the Lord has made. Let us rejoice and be glad in it!"

That was enough to get most of the attention off me in time for me to get to my seat. But I could still feel everyone's eyes on me, hear the whispering, and see the pointing and the shaking of heads in my peripheral. I was unfazed by them. I was on a mission to worship and fulfill my duties as First Lady. Service went on without a hitch, but the atmosphere still seemed a little heavy. Everyone had to have some semblance of knowledge of what happened last Wednesday whether they were there or not and of course that was the main contributor to this spirit of heaviness in the air. It was so thick I could cut it with a knife. I tried not to let it get to me, but I couldn't help it. I was the closest one to the flame and of course I was burnt, but I didn't want them to see that. I had to be strong and maintain my image and that of their pastor in his absence. This was a thorny situation, and I didn't really have anyone I could talk to or confide in there at New Salem. I was alone and isolated in this situation where I knew what I had to do but was hesitant to execute for some unknown reason.

I was pulled from my thoughts when the presiding deacon asked if I had any words from the pulpit. My heart skipped a beat. I wasn't prepared and I had no intention to address the congregation that day, but all eyes were on me, so I had to say something. I rose to my feet, smoothed out my skirt, and made my way to the podium with the congregation applauding as I came. "Praise the Lord," I said once I was behind the podium. I paused to look into the crowd where I saw the faces of most of the women who had been at Wednesday night Bible study the week before. They knew the whole story and my predicament. I knew in that moment that I would have to be very careful with my words. I pursed my lips and looked down at an empty podium. There were no notes, no script. This was all me.

"Thank you for your prayers, phone calls, and words of encouragement. They are much appreciated. All I ask is that you please continue to keep me and Bishop Black in your prayers at this time. With God's help, we'll make it through this. Thank you."

The congregation applauded and there were a few "amens" and "hallelujahs" as I returned to my seat. I think what I said was appropriate enough. I mean, what else could I have said? I had some work to do, but I would need some major help doing it.

By Friday, I had reached my breaking point. As quiet and peaceful as the house had been with Bishop gone, it had become my own personal hell. Every room held a memory or some reminder of him. Things had gotten so crazy with the press that I was now afraid to leave the house, so I chose to stay holed up there. I had my groceries delivered and I even decided to work from home for a while.

L. C. was concerned – dare I say suspicious, but he allowed it. When church members would drop by to check on me, I didn't answer the door. I felt myself sinking and I knew talking to someone would help me, but I didn't have anyone available. Most of the church members were acquaintances, my colleagues at work were off limits, and I definitely couldn't tell David even though he said he would be there for me if I needed him. I was really in this all by myself...or so I thought. Then I remembered Anita and how she'd helped me make sense of things before. So, I gave her a call.

I was greeted with a warm, "Hello, Brooke. It's been a while. How are you?"

"I'm..." *Be honest, now.* "I'm not doing well, Anita." I went on to relay everything that had happened since that fateful Wednesday night up until the present moment. Anita listened intently and never stopped me or interrupted me while I poured out my heart over the phone. I ended with, "I know that was a lot, but I had nowhere else to turn or anyone else I could talk to. What should I do, Anita?"

"You know what you need to do, Brooke," Anita replied. "You need to do the thing that's scaring you most right now. But first, you need to address everything that stands between you and that. Once you get past those obstacles, you'll be able to handle your business. Right now, fear seems to be the elephant in the room. What are you afraid of, Brooke? What is keeping you from doing the thing that will make you free?"

I paused. Deep down, I knew she was right. Anita always had a way of reading me like a book and pulling out all the suppressed or undiscovered truths I held inside. "I'm afraid - I'm afraid of peoples' opinions… losing face…and embarrassment," I choked.

"That's good and completely normal. But let me ask you, do peoples' opinions make you who you are? Do peoples' opinions determine your joy, happiness or peace? Does losing face and the embarrassment that comes with that disqualify you from living the life you deserve?"

"No, no, and no."

"Then, what makes you who you are? What will enable you to experience inner peace, be happy, and have joy? What entitles you to live the life you absolutely deserve?"

"I remember how we talked about all of this before. It was different, and it was a long time ago.

But the gist was that I need to stop denying myself what will make me happy. I owe it to myself to take the next step and go through with this divorce."

"There she is," Anita said proudly. I could hear the smile in her voice. "I think I know a good divorce lawyer or two out your way. I could forward you their information if you'd like."

"I would! Thank you, Anita. I'm so glad I met you on that plane!"

Anita chuckled. "It's my pleasure, Soror. Whether it was by chance or divine intervention, it was meant to happen."

About an hour after I got off the phone with Anita, I looked in my inbox and she'd actually sent me a list of a few divorce lawyers in my area. *So much for one or two*, I thought, but was grateful, nonetheless. All I had to do was pick one and get this ball rolling. But I had to be discreet in the execution of my plan.

I sat in the chair in front of my would-be lawyer's desk, listening to some oldies softly pumping through speakers in the ceiling. He was four, soon to be five minutes late for our appointment. I sighed in frustration as I started to regret my decision to go with this one, who had such high reviews. Then he came in, obviously flustered from rushing to get back on time. Despite my disappointment with his tardiness, I stood and extended my hand for a handshake. He was shocked by the gesture but gave me a firm handshake in return. After he apologized for being late and we exchanged pleasantries, we got down to business. He said that he reviewed my case and came to the conclusion that I had a "clear case of extreme cruelty."

I couldn't believe my ears. Did I hear him correctly? "When you say 'clear,' do you mean apparent?"

"Yes, ma'am," he replied. "The evidence is plain as day."

I didn't hear whatever else he had to say because I'd disappeared into my own thoughts. *Wait a minute?* I thought. *Have I lost my mind – my senses? You mean to tell me that all these years, I've come up with reasons, rationalizing, making excuses, and explaining away this fool's reckless behavior when all the while the extreme cruelty has been APPARENT?*

I was brought back by the sound of Johnny Mathis' voice crooning, *Guess it's over, call it a day...Sorry that it had to end this way.* In that moment, I only had one thing on my mind. "Where are the papers and where do I sign?" I asked. It was high time I had made this move. I was long overdue to start working toward my happiness, inner peace, and living the life I truly deserved. ...*No reason to pretend...We knew it had to end someday, this way...*

Chapter 20

Intimate Strangers

Day 1: Bishop's Back

After his antics when I first announced I wanted a divorce, you'd think that Bishop would go to even greater extremes to try and change my mind once I'd served the papers. Much to my surprise, he just took them. No fuss, no fight – just silence. I wasn't sure if he was trying to be peaceful or if he was simply trying to gauge how I would react so he could use it as ammunition for when he revealed his bigger, better plot to try and change my mind. Nonetheless, I had wised up to him by now. Call me cocky, but I can smell bull from a mile away and he reeked of it. I just had to watch and wait for the next trick he'd try to pull.

24 Hours Earlier

I had just come back into my home office after running downstairs to fix myself some tea when I noticed that I had a voicemail message. I checked the missed call notification and didn't recognize the number. It wasn't marked as spam or fraudulent, so I listened to the message. I'm glad I had put down my tea. Otherwise, I would've had to buy a new laptop. Bishop had called and he was oh so happy to announce that he'd made bail and would be on his way home in just a few hours. I replayed the message once and again just to be sure that this was for real. I guess it really was. I deleted the message before sinking into my chair. I was expecting this day to come, but not so soon. I was starting to get used to the peace, quiet, and solitude. Now that he was coming home, I realized most if not, all of that would disappear much like the woman I was before this dreadful marriage.

I pinched the bridge of my nose and sighed, "Why me? Why now?" My thoughts began to race as I pictured different scenarios of when he got home. Did I want to be here? Should I leave now? If I leave, when should I come back? Should I post up in a hotel for the night? Or the week? *Hold up, pause.* When have I ever been one to back down from a challenge? There's no way I could ever see myself running away from this. I was a lawyer for goodness' sake – and on the verge of making partner at my firm. How dare I even consider leaving *my* house just because my getting-out-of-jail, soon-to-be ex-husband was being released.

I took a deep breath, counted to ten, and exhaled. *You've got this, Brooke. Remember what Anita said. You've got to do the thing that scares you the most. You've got the papers…now you just have to serve them.* I always had a flare for the dramatic, but as much as I wanted to be extra with serving the papers, I decided a clean and direct approach was best.

Day 6: Back to New Salem

The Sunday Bishop returned to New Salem was much more dreadful to me than the Sunday I had to go on my own after that fateful Wednesday night. Of course, he insisted that we go together because what would the people think if we arrived in separate cars on the day of his triumphal return to the pulpit? The scandal! He even went so far as to suggest that we could rock matching color outfits. That was a line I refused to cross. So, he reverted to insisting we ride together. He would not take "no" for an answer, so that's how I wound up in the passenger seat while we made our way to Sunday service. The tension in the air was heavier than any weighted blanket. Neither one of us said a word. We simply rode in silence.

When we pulled up the to the church, I was ready to bolt the moment the car came to a complete stop, but once again, I had to maintain the image of *The Good Wife*. As irritating as it was, I willed myself to wait for Bishop to get out of the car, smile and wave at some passing saints, stride around the front of the car, open my door, and help me out of the car. And thus, began our grandest performance to date.

When it was all said and done, I couldn't believe how well I managed to smile, grin, wave, keep my mouth shut, and let Bishop do all the talking. I sat amazed at how he effortlessly managed to evade questions, redirect conversations, and charm his way back into the hearts of most of the congregants. This man was beyond despicable and I hated to admit that I had loved him at one point in time. I mean, he was so good that he deserved a Golden Globe. He fronted that he wasn't fazed by all the attention he was getting, but he was *living* for it.

He had them hanging on his every word as he thanked God, the clergy, the congregation, the city council, his team, his supporters, and last but not least, little ole me – his beautiful, kind, strong, loving, and supportive wife of so many years for standing by his side throughout this whole ordeal. I might have been smiling on the outside, but honey, on the inside, I was thinking, *Phew! Negro, if they only knew HALF of what I knew, you wouldn't be enjoying ANY of what you've got going on right now. But that's all right. Enjoy your time in the sun because night is well on its way.*

Present Day

It has been three weeks and a day since that Sunday. The way Bishop and I do life now is nothing like I pictured it would be back when we first got married. Back then, we were so in love that nothing could separate us. Now, we're the equivalent of roommates; we have become two separate entities who just so happen to share the same living space. I stay in what used to be our bedroom while he stays in the guest room. I've even stopped cooking meals for two. Bishop was hotter than fish grease the first few times I did that, but I suppose he's grown to accept it as he sobs into his Chinese take-out.

But let it be Sunday morning service, Wednesday night Bible study, the occasional second service, or a city council function; the spotlight comes on, everyone is staring, so we smile, wave, grin, and act like we love each other for the masses. It makes me sick to put on my mask every Sunday and Wednesday, every Wednesday and Sunday, or anytime I have to…But I do it anyway.

As the days dragged on, it started to feel like this was all life had to offer me; that this was how things would be and I'd never get out of this endless game of make believe. But then one day when I was scrolling on Instagram, I saw a graphic that said, "Trust the process." I don't know if it was the background, the colors, or the font that caught my eye, but I stared at that graphic for almost two minutes. And there wasn't a caption! *Is this a sign? Nah.* Then I went about my day only to get a text from Anita with a different graphic, but the same phrase. I was tempted to ask for context, but she texted again before I could ask with: "Thought you could use this today!" I thanked her, but still didn't have enough sense to see it as a sign.

It wasn't until later that evening when I was about to search for a hair tutorial that I saw it. Before I even clicked the search bar, I saw a video entitled, "Trust the Process." I had to take a moment to process. I closed my laptop and rested my chin in my hand. After a beat, I opened the laptop only to see that the video was still there. This was the third time today that I saw that phrase. You can't tell me it wasn't a sign. Besides, there has always been something about the number 3. I've seen it appear all throughout my life in different ways – mostly before turning points or during difficult times. I don't claim to subscribe to numerology, but to me, this *had* to be a sign.

At that moment, I realized that my current situation wasn't the end of the road. I had way too many hopes, dreams, and ambitions for my life to amount to nothing but playing a role that I wasn't made to fill. I was meant for much more than this. I'd taken the initial steps. All I needed to do was hang in for the ride and wait for everything to come together, which I knew would happen sooner or later. I just needed to trust the process. No. I needed to trust God to lead and bring me through this long and tiring process. Because there's no way I'm going to make it through all this on my strength alone. *Just gotta keep it together. Remember why you started the process and keep that at the front of your mind. Things* ***will*** *work out.*

~~~

One day, Bishop and I got into an argument over the phone. I'd like to think it was over the fact that he cancelled yet another visit with Stephan and Stephanie, but then again, it might have been over nothing. We had our share of passive-aggressive fights and a few screaming matches since he'd been home, but today was the day for a screaming match. And Bishop was just about done with me, but I wasn't finished with him.

"Don't you DARE hang up on me, Bishop!" I yelled.

"You're lucky I have an incoming call, woman."

"Send it to voice mail!"

"I have to take this."

"Don't-,"

"Hey, baby," he said in that sweet, make-you-melt-like-butter voice he used to use on me.

Say what now?! I was faced with a major decision here. I could either play along or go off...I opted for the latter. "BABY?! WHO THE HELL IS BABY, BISHOP? AIN'T NO BABY HERE!"

"Oh, shoot," Bishop mumbled.

"I AM YOUR GODDAMN WIFE! SINCE WHEN HAVE YOU EVER CALLED ME BA- Hello? Bishop?" I pulled the phone away from my ear to see that the phone call ended. *This negro really done hung up on me. That's fine. Because he's gotta come home at some point.*

Bishop didn't come home until a little after 8 that night. I was sitting in the living room waiting for him to arrive in my white silk robe – the kind a rich woman would wear after her husband died mysteriously – and matching slides. I commended him in my mind for how hard he tried to be quiet when opening and closing the door, but I heard him regardless. Before he could take one step toward the stairs, I said, "So, who's Baby?" I heard him sigh irritably. So, I came to lean against the door post and asked again, "Who's Baby?"

He was obviously thrown off by the clash between my outfit and my demeanor, but he was done in more ways than one. "I'm not talking about this, Brooke."

He tried to make his way to the stairs, but I blocked his path. He easily could have pushed me aside, but he didn't. "No, I wanna know. Who's this Baby you addressed during our argument earlier this afternoon?"

"It's nobody," he mumbled. "Now, please move. It's been a long day and I'm tired."

"Oh, I bet you are!" I said as I patted him on the cheek. "You've had a long day of avoiding coming home because you knew you'd have to deal with me, right? So, what? Do I have to play the guessing game?"

"Drop it, Brooke," he said through gritted teeth.

"Still not gonna budge, huh? It'd be so much easier if you'd just tell me who she is and confirm what I already know."

"YOU KNOW NOTHING!" he growled.

"Like your followers and many blind supporters? You don't think I saw Kelly chasing after you that Wednesday night? The slut was wearing *YOUR* shirt, genius!" I scoffed at how dumb he thought I was. "You know what? It's cool. You don't have to tell me anything. Just do us both a favor and crawl back to Kelly because you're not staying here tonight."

"What're you talking about? Of course, I'm st-,"

"No, you're not," I said so calmly, yet so firmly that even I couldn't tell if it was just a statement or a threat.

Bishop didn't want to find out, so he just backed off and left without another word.

I stood my ground until the headlights from his car were gone from sight. Then I locked the front door, went to the kitchen, poured myself a glass of wine, and savored it right there. I couldn't believe that he didn't make a move to touch me that whole time. There's no telling what would have happened had he done so. I was just happy that he was gone and that I had the house to myself at least for one night.

When I finished the glass of wine, I looked at the bottle I left sitting on the counter as I contemplated what my next move would be. I simply shrugged, grabbed the glass and bottle, and went upstairs. Since Bishop was gone, I thought I'd make the most of it. I nestled into bed with a book I had gotten but never started, and dove right in. But only after I turned on my reading playlist and let the tunes fill the air of my sanctuary.

About five pages later, a song came on that touched my soul. It got so good to me that I had to mark my page and put my book aside so I could properly appreciate it. Who else, but Patti Labelle and Michael McDonald would speak to the events of this day? ...*By myself, On my own*... At that moment, I was home alone, enjoying my own company....*I've got to find out where I belong again, I've got to learn to be strong again*... I still had my power, evidenced by how I confronted Bishop about who this Baby really was despite the fact we both knew. ...*I never dreamed I'd spend one night alone...By myself, by myself, by myself...*

As I sat and intentionally listened to the words, I realized that yes, I needed this time with myself and for myself because I truly needed to cancel all the noise that was Bishop, the role of *The Good Wife*, and everything that just wasn't for me. ...*I've got to find out what was mine again...My heart is saying that it's time again...* This was my time to refocus on who I was and what I wanted, rebuild what was left of the woman I was, and reinforce the aspects of the woman I was becoming.

...*And I have faith that I will shine again...* The sun would rise again. ...*By myself...* And I would have my time to stand on the shores of solitude.

Chapter 21

It's All Her Fault

"We can't keep meeting like this," Kelly grumbled as she fought a flyaway strand of hair that just wouldn't lay right.

"You've never complained before," Bishop said as he came to stand behind her in the mirror, adjusting his tie.

Kelly let out an exasperated sigh as she gave up the fight with her hair. "I'm sick of being the side piece. Why don't you just leave Brooke? Your relationship is dead. Bury it and move on."

"It's not that simple, Kelly. We've been over this."

"Yeah, yeah, I know. You have an image to maintain as the perfect first family. Got it," Kelly said with a roll of her eyes and shake of her head.

"Well, it's not like you'd be the perfect first lady, either."

"Excuse me, I'm ten times the first lady Brooke is or could *ever* be."

Bishop slipped his hands in his pockets and leaned against the vanity. "When you're meeting me in different hotels on a bi-weekly basis? That's questionable."

Kelly, not wanting to admit he was right, grabbed her makeup bag and started to beat her face. Bishop sat on the bed and watched her in the mirror for a few minutes before saying, "So, about this wedding that's coming up-,"

Kelly had been waiting for him to bring it up. "I'm sorry, Baby, but you're gonna have to miss out on this one."

He looked almost insulted when he heard her say that. "What? Why?"

"The bride said so."

"A-Are you sure?" he stammered, struggling to accept the fact that he wasn't invited to not just any wedding, but THE wedding. A dear friend of his from way back was getting married on one of the most beautiful beaches in the world and he was going to miss it simply because the bride said so? He wasn't about to take that laying down. "I can't even be your plus one?"

"Did I stutter? There was no indication of plus one on the announcement or invitation."

"Yeah, but that doesn't mean she *won't* allow a plus one. Come on, Kelly. Sweetheart, could you at least try to put in a good word for me?" Bishop came up behind her to rub on her shoulders.

She was getting tired of this conversation. "I did. And she said no. Besides, that wife of yours wouldn't make it easy for us to get together if you were to go, anyway." *That should be the end of it*, she thought.

"Brooke was invited?" "…

Yep," Kelly said flatly.

"She didn't tell me anything about a wedding…" Again, with the devastated, almost insulted look on his face.

"Go with her! You could use the break from here anyway. Kick back and relax."

"I'd like it much better if I was kicking back and relaxing in Jamaica with *you*."

"Yeah, but that's not an option now, *is* it?" She paused to look at the clock. "You really ought to get going. Don't you have a meeting in…30 minutes?"

"You're right, I should go," Bishop said as he got up and got his freshly pressed suit jacket from the closet. "But do you think you could ask her again?" he asked, making one last attempt to work his charm.

"Bishop," Kelly sighed as she spritzed the final touch of setting spray before setting it aside, "I asked Michelle twice. The answer was no both times. What makes you think she'd change her mind this time?"

He sucked his teeth. "Did she at least say why?"

That's a new tone, Kelly thought. "N-No, she didn't."

"Don't lie to me, Kelly."

Now, she was really scared of the tone he was using with her. All her hairs were standing on end and she had a knot in her stomach. She needed to get him out and quick. "Okay, okay," she said as she abruptly got up from the vanity and put a little distance between herself and Bishop. "She said it was because of the scandal."

"WHAT?!" Bishop yelled. "For the love of God, really?"

"Her words, not mine!"

"That's just it – It was a scandal! Nothing more, nothing less."

"But people aren't stupid, Bishop! They *can* read between the lines."

"You know what? This is all *your* fault," Bishop said as he jabbed a finger in her face. "If you hadn't been at the church when the cops busted in that night, my nose would still be clean."

"MY FAULT? Please! If you had been a man and handled your business, you wouldn't have those child support charges against you!" Kelly shot back. She interpreted his silence to mean that she'd won. *Shall I go further?* "And if you were able to keep it in your pants-," Next thing she knew, Bishop had her by the throat and pinned against the wall.

"That's enough out of you," he growled. "Now give me one good reason why I shouldn't be the Ike to your Tina."

Is this really happening right now? Kelly thought as she stared into the stone-cold eyes of a stranger who was her lover only a few minutes prior. *Should I fight? No. There's no way I could win. I know, I'll scream.*

"Scream and I'll squeeze," he said before she could take a breath. It was almost as if he'd read her mind. "I'm waiting for my answer."

This was the first time she'd ever seen this side of Bishop and it was unsettling to say the least – No. It was terrifying. She'd never been in a position like this before where her words alone could save her or compromise her even further.

"B-Because I'm gonna ask Michelle to let you be my plus one one more time and I'll make sure she does. Promise." She offered a weak smile, despite the fact that her voice shook with every word she spoke.

Bishop paused to consider, neither tightening nor loosening his grip around her neck. "Hm…You know, that would've been a good answer IF I actually believed you were able to accomplish such a feat."

"But, I ca-,"

"No, Kelly. If you *were* capable, we wouldn't be having this conversation right now. You said I have a meeting in 30? Well, that leaves me at least 10 to remind you who's running this show."

"Wha-? Bishop, no, PLEASE!"

One blow turned to two. Two blows turned to three. After that, Kelly lost count as she made futile attempts to shield herself from the onslaught of kicks and punches. All this over what? A denied request for a plus one to the destination wedding of the century. *How on earth did it come to this?* Kelly thought. *Where were the signs? Were they ever there? Did I even stop to look?* She begged and pleaded for him to stop, but her cries went unanswered for the 10 longest minutes of her life.

Then the vicious attack came to an end. Bishop left without a word as Kelly lay curled in a ball on the floor, afraid to move for fear that he would return and pick up where he left off. Once she convinced herself that Bishop wasn't coming back, she found the strength to crawl to the nightstand where her phone was charging and call her job to inform them that she wouldn't be coming in that day. When she hung up and went to put the phone back, she accidentally pulled up Pandora and the intro to a classic tune started to play. She really wasn't in the mood for music, but she didn't have the energy to turn it off, so she let it play out. ... *But then she's gone, you're all alone...* This incident was the first and last time Bishop would ever lay his hands on her. The hopelessly in love woman she was before was gone and Bishop would soon be alone.

"I saw Kelly the other day," Cathy mentioned, knowing I couldn't care less about what or who that chick was doing.

I glared at her through slit eyes. Normally, I'd change the subject, but the way she mentioned it out of nowhere had me wondering, *Why?* So, I asked, "What about her?"

"She was wearing bug eye sunglasses on an overcast day, a long sleeve blouse in 70 plus-degree weather, and sporting a pair of flats." My jaw dropped. "Mm-hm…She wouldn't be caught dead in flats. She's known for her proclivity for heels."

"Preach," I said as I raised my glass and took a sip.

"If it's less than 5 inches, she won't wear it."

"So true," I chuckled while Cathy got quiet. I felt the change in the mood. There was clearly a reason why she was saying this. I put my glass down, leaned in closer, and asked, "Why'd you ask me here today, Cathy?"

Cathy looked at me with a grave expression on her face. "I know you're trying to leave Bishop."

How?! I started to panic because I'd been so diligent – so careful to keep it under wraps, yet she still managed to find out? Was it that obvious? When and where did I slip up?

"It's not obvious. But I'm not the only one who knows."

I looked around the café to make sure no one was listening. "Who else knows?"

"…Ask Mother Evans. She sees and knows things many people tend to miss. I know she can come across as judgmental, but she's a very sweet and wise woman. She earned those gray hairs on her head."

"…I'm sure she did."

I wasn't sure how to approach Mother about Bishop or our situation without telling her outright what was going on. The crazy thing is, I didn't even have to approach her. She called me three days later at almost 5 am. She apologized and told me she had a dream. In the dream, she saw me stretched out in a casket for all to see and mourn. Bishop was also in the dream, but he was not moved at all. While everyone else was weeping, he sat on the front pew indifferent. She went on to tell me that she was dreaming in black and white until Bishop came into the dream, but he was outlined in red. And everything he touched became red, as well. The conversation ended with her telling me that I needed to get out and get away quickly. I wasn't one to subscribe to visions or dreams of that nature, but this chilled me to the bone. So much so that I was ready to do whatever was necessary to protect myself.

I'd always hoped against hope that the Ryan I knew and loved would come back to me, but Mother Evans seemed to know a darker, more menacing force was at work here and I wasn't willing to take any chances with my life.

Chapter 22

When People Show the World

I was sitting in my office a few days after my conversation with Mother Evans, trying to focus on doing all that I needed to do concerning Bishop, but something was stopping me. It wasn't fear. I think it was my desire to be as discreet as possible. I didn't want any blowback messing with my career, and I was concerned about the congregation. Somehow, I still thought if I could give them a Golden Globe worthy performance as *The Good Wife*, it would give them some sense of normalcy through the separation. Maybe I was overthinking it. Maybe I just had to do what I had to do.

I let out a sigh, took off my glasses, and pinched the bridge of my nose. It was then that I decided to take a jog. *I need to get out and clear my mind...Maybe this will help*, I thought. It had before. I changed out of my business casual and into a cute purple and pink jogging suit I'd been dying to wear for a workout. Grabbed my keys, phone, and water bottle then I left for the park.

After I finished stretching, I started my run. When I tuned up my running playlist, as fate would have it, or so they say, a song that spoke directly to my situation started to play...*She's just a girl, and she's on fire*... I had so much going on – so many things on my mind. ...*She's living in a world, and it's on fire*... The church, my career, and this legal union because I couldn't call it a marriage anymore. ...*Filled with catastrophe, but she knows she can fly away*... I knew what I had to do, but there's a major difference between knowing what you need to do and following through.

I had to give myself some credit, though. I stood up to Bishop and put him out that one time he called me Baby when he meant to call Kelly by that pet name. I had gone to a divorce lawyer, got the papers in order, and served them. Everything was in motion, but there was more that needed to be done. *Why are you hesitating?* I thought to myself. I suppose part of me was still clinging to the hope that maybe – just maybe things would work out, somehow the marriage would survive, Ryan and I would be happy again, and we'd be able to pursue the life we always wanted and give Daddy the one thing he always wanted.

My mind wandered to Daddy. It had been a minute since we last spoke, much less saw each other and it hurt me to admit that. I wasn't so busy that I could forget my own father…was I? *No way.* I purposed that I would call him sometime soon. I thought I might even pay him and Mommy a visit.

The next thing that came to mind as I was closing in on my first half mile was my career. I loved my job, my firm, my boss, and got along with *most* of my coworkers. I wanted to hang in to see if I made partner since L.C. had hinted that I was so close to making it and needed to only be patient and stay the course. But how long would I have to wait? I should've *been* partner with all the cases I closed, time and effort I invested, and all the collaboration with the "team." I was putting my blood, sweat, and tears into this firm only to have my just due dangled before me like a carrot.

This frustrated me to no end, but while I was willing to wait and see what the end would be, part of me was entertaining the idea of starting my own practice. I had the skill, the resources, and the ability to move and connect with people in certain spaces that L.C. and others at the firm could not.

Decisions needed to be made; not exactly at that moment, but I seriously needed to sit down and weigh all my options, pros, cons, and motives before making any moves.

I was just about to wrap up my run when I got a call. Normally, I would have let it go to voicemail, but this wasn't just anybody calling. I had to take it, so I paused at a bench and decided to stretch while I talked. "Talk to me, Dex."

"Brooke, we've been over this," Dex replied, annoyed by the nickname I gave him.

"I'm sorry, I'm sorry. Let me start over." I got into my professional headspace. *Scene.* "Hi, Dexter. Is that better?"

"Very much better, thank you. I'm calling because I have some news for you."

"News? Did you need me to come into the office?"

"You don't have to, but you could swing by if you'd like."

I thought about it. "No, you can just tell me over the phone."

"Very well, then. I'm calling in regard to Bishop or R-,"

"Ryan Black, yes, yes. Cut to the chase." I didn't mean to sound pushy, but any news about Bishop was most likely not good news and I wanted to deal with it sooner rather than later. I also wanted to finish my run.

"A report against him has been brought to my attention and is currently being investigated."

"Okay…what kind of report and who was it made by?"

"Give me one second…The report was for assault and it was made by one…Kelly Wilson." I nearly dropped my phone at the mention of her name. After a long pause, Dexter asked, "Brooke, are you alright?"

"Y-Yeah," I stammered, still a little shaken up by how real everything just got.

"Do you know Ms. Wilson?"

"I've only met her in passing…but she just so happens to be my husband's side piece."

"Noted. According to the hospital record, she sustained quite a few injuries as the result of a beating – Two black eyes, a busted lip, three cracked ribs, a sprained ankle and wrist, and multiple bruises all over her body."

I couldn't help but go back to my wedding night as I listened to him name her injuries. My heart went out to her even though she was what most would say, my enemy. But since she had made this report, she unknowingly became my ally in the fight against our now mutual enemy, Bishop.

"With all this in mind," Dexter continued, "I would advise you to put him out for your own safety, maybe even get a restraining order."

"Yes," I said without hesitation. "Yes, to all that. I'll get on it as soon as I'm off the phone."

"That won't be necessary. The only thing you'll need to do is pack his bags and ship them wherever he'll be staying."

"Wait, what do you mean?" I asked. "What won't be necessary?"

"Where are you now?"

"I-I'm at the park on a run."

"And where is Bishop?"

"At the house, why?" He wasn't making any sense.

"Hm…Okay. I was asking because I can make arrangements for both the restraining order and for the locks to be changed at your house, but I know you want to be discreet. I can either put a rush on the restraining order or wait until you provide me with a date for the locks so the two coincide."

"Um…" My mind was swimming. This was a lot to take in at once. I closed my eyes and paused for a minute to think through this as to find the best solution to all the problems. I knew Bishop would be leaving for a four-day leadership conference out of town, so that would work. "Okay, how about we change the locks on… Thursday."

"Sounds good. Now, for me to get started on the restraining order, all I would need is your verbal consent."

"Yes."

"Excellent. That's all I had to report. Do you have any questions for me before I go, Brooke?"

"…I don't have a question, but I *would* like to say thank you." Dexter had done me a few solids in the past, but not like this. I was truly grateful for all the work he was doing, not only to keep me safe, but to help me win this case.

"You're very welcome, Brooke. You take care, now."

"Thanks. You too, Dexter."

As soon as I hung up, I sank onto the bench I'd been pacing around during the entire conversation with Dexter and just took a moment to breathe. All this time, I've been agonizing over the things I would have to do… Everything just got handled in a single phone call. *Thank You, Jesus*, I thought as I looked up to the sky. I couldn't help but think, *Wow.*

My life was literally on the line because of this man's unpredictable violent streak. I thought back to all the signs and warnings I dismissed, fought, and ignored from the time I met Bishop up until now. My parents warned me and I didn't listen. Pastor Townes warned me and I didn't listen. Most recently, Mother Evans told me and I was convinced. But after this call from Dexter and what I already knew from Cathy, I don't need any more convincing. I have seen and know way too much for me to continue staying in this relationship, much less the same house as this man. He had "DANGER" written all over him from the start, but I was too blind to see. I could just kick myself about it, but love is blind, or so they say.

Now, I am done. Done playing *The Good Wife* – done smiling, grinning, charming, and lying to people. Bishop had shown me and the world the type of man he was. He'd slipped up not once, but twice in the public eye. *His* decisions and *his* actions put him in this predicament. I was in no way, shape, or form responsible for covering for him, trying to clear his name, or save face. Bishop was all by himself. As far as I was concerned, I was that girl on fire Alicia Keys was singing about. I was surrounded by catastrophe, but I had all the wherewithal I needed to fly far, far away.

Chapter 23

Growing Pains

I couldn't help but let out a cheer as I spun victoriously in my office chair. I had just completed the draft of my letter of resignation. After some deep thought, I decided that I ought to start my own practice. It might sound strange, but it felt like I was being called to do so. It wasn't me or my ambition that drew me to this idea. It was beyond me. I've heard it said that each person's purpose is an answer to a problem for someone somewhere in the world. I guess my practice was going to be someone's answer – an answer that no other firm in the area could provide. *Now, to save it as a draft*, I thought as I consciously clicked 'save draft.' The last thing I needed was to accidentally send it to L.C. before I had everything in place. I only needed 2 more things before I could send that email: (1) a location; and (2) a date.

Luckily, I had been looking at different locations beforehand. A few had gone off the market, but not so many that I couldn't find some places I liked. There were at least three buildings I had my eye on. If I could narrow it down to two, then choose, I would be happy. As for my date of resignation, it all depended on how soon I could secure a location, make it to my liking, and open it. There was time for all that.

Not even two seconds after I'd logged out of my email, Mike Jr. came slinking into my office to make small talk. I had neither the patience, nor kindness of heart to entertain him. It was obvious he was being nosy and trying to get whatever scoop he could to use against me in his bid to make partner. Sad for him, he had nothing on me and little did he know I was planning to leave. But I wasn't about to let him know that. Then he'd have an actual reason to make my life on the job hell until I made my exit. So, I politely excused myself for lunch, and scooted him out as I left.

I went to a little taquería a few blocks down from the firm and treated myself to a Mexican with the works because I was hungry. As I ate, I was going back and forth between the three properties I was considering. I could see myself at any one of them, but I wanted to settle on one and have it be my forever space – my mark, my baby, my legacy – complete with longevity and room for expansion. By the time lunch was over, there was one less location on the table.

Later that night, I was overcome by an overwhelming sense of urgency to settle on a location. I don't know if it was a divine prompt, my ambition, or what it could've been. All I know is that it was hitting me. But I had to take a step back because I didn't want to make any rash decisions out of fear, desperation, or impatience. I had thought and prayed about opening my own practice in the past but took a more intentional approach more recently, and the way things were going, it looked like God was in this. So, I went to bed calm and at ease, knowing my path was set and I would emerge victorious.

I awoke shaking in a cold sweat. *A nightmare?* I thought once I assessed my surroundings and grounded myself. I turned on the light and squinted at the light before closing my eyes once and again to adjust to the brightness. The sight of a burning building and gun-wielding Bishop flashed across my mind. I rubbed my eyes before I got out of bed and made my way to the bathroom.

I turned on the light, hobbled to the sink, turned on the water and splashed some cold water on my face. When I looked in the mirror after drying my face, I saw Bishop staring back at me with a knife to my neck and I let out a scream as I squeezed my eyes shut. I knew it wasn't real. It was residue from the nightmare, but in that moment, I was the most scared I'd ever been in my life. Once I had quieted my breathing, I found the courage to open my eyes again. I opened one eye at first then opened the other once I saw it was just my own reflection in the mirror.

I leaned against the sink, took a long look at myself in that mirror, and said, "You…are *definitely* on the right track."

I couldn't help but wonder if there was some deeper hidden meaning to this nightmare. Was it a vision, a sick compilation of all I had been facing lately, or a tactic of the enemy to try and scare me out of fulfilling my purpose? Judging by the timing, I would say it was undoubtedly a tactic. I might have been shaken, but I was not moved by this. Starting my practice was something I had to do. If I wasn't sure before, I was sure now. This nightmare confirmed that much for me.

I went back to bed with a renewed sense of purpose and slept with one light on while my worship tunes played softly and ushered me into more pleasant dreams. The last thing I remember before fading completely was Jessica Reedy making a declaration over my situation ...*It gets better, better, better.*

After that night was when the real tests began. It started with minor inconveniences like me spilling coffee on my blouse or forgetting my wallet. Then it escalated about a week later and expanded into the firm. Tensions were high, tempers were short, and folk were feeling froggy over the littlest thing. Even L.C. was starting to wonder what was going on. I knew exactly what the root of the issue was, but I couldn't tell him anything. Not yet. Not until I had secured my space.

Then came the caseloads that nearly made it impossible for me to even have time to consider my two remaining locations. I had meeting after meeting, hearing after hearing, this social, that social, and the like. By the time I had set aside to consider my practice came around, I was too beat to even bother. Everything seemed to be going against me and the boundaries I set in place so that I could have a healthy work-life balance and thrive. It just seemed like I was trying to survive until the weekend where I didn't have to answer any phone calls, send any emails, or do any consultations.

When the weekend came around, all I wanted to do was rest; breathe, do some yoga, drink a glass of wine, and chill. Maybe even bother David if I felt up to it. I had shared my desire to start my own practice with him before and he wholeheartedly supported my decision. According to him, I was made to be my own boss and call my own shots. I'd spent too much time working for someone else to be put on a waiting list. My time to shine was now. All I had to do was get my ducks in order and make it happen.

I didn't chew pens before, but I was certainly chewing them now as I was anxiously awaiting either one or two things from L.C.: (1) a response to my letter of resignation; or (2) a request to meet in his office. I had sent my email on Friday morning, went all day and the entire weekend without hearing anything, and here it is almost time for lunch on Monday and I *still* haven't heard a word. *Was this a mistake?* I thought. *Am I leaving too soon? What is he thinking? How will he-?*

I heard my email ping. I got a new message from L.C. I didn't even have to open it. The subject line was all I needed to read. It read: A Word?

I sighed and resigned myself to my fate. This man wanted to meet face-to-face. I had never been more anxious in my life. I got up and paced about my office for a minute all while taking deep breaths. Then I made my way out of my office, down the halls, and to L.C.'s office. It might have looked like I was walking with purpose, but every step I took felt like I had cinderblocks chained to my ankles.

When I reached his door, it was wide open. His door was never open. I couldn't tell if this was a good or bad sign. All I knew was that it wasn't helping the already erratic beating of my heart.

Before I could knock, L.C. said, "Come on in, Brooke."

I took a deep breath then stepped into his office. Much to my surprise, I was met by a cork that nearly hit my nose. L.C. apologized as he poured two glasses of champagne – Definitely not what I was expecting at all. He handed me a glass and urged me to have a seat before he went to close the door.

Once he returned to his seat behind the desk, he said, "You took me by surprise, Brooke. But then again, I'm not so surprised. I've kept you waiting far too long."

"You make it sound like you were trying to get me to start my own practice all along, L.C."

"That was never my intention. You have all it takes to become partner and more. I'm just upset I didn't offer it to you before…well, this. I hate to see you go," he sighed, "but I'm sure you will do great and marvelous things. You see, very few people leave this firm once they get here because they think this is all there is. But you? You've got something they don't."

"And what's that?" I asked.

"You have the skill. You have the talent. You have the ambition. And you have the passion for this line of work. But most importantly, you have a sense of purpose, Brooke. That's something so many others like you *wish* they had."

I raised an eyebrow. "If that's the case, then why *didn't* you make me partner?"

"Well," he began in a way that made it seem like he was about to make a major confession, "I suppose I knew that you were meant for greater than partner and I didn't want to tether you to something that was good for the firm but not great for you."

I was speechless. L.C. Westbrook, a WHITE MAN, just told me, a BLACK WOMAN, that he knew I wasn't cut out to be a *mere partner* when I could run my own practice. I couldn't believe my ears.

"Th-Thank you." I didn't mean to stammer, but I was just so moved hearing that statement directly from him. "I didn't know you thought so highly of me."

"Well, now you know. Let's toast to great success, longevity, and health to you and your firm."

"Hear! Hear!"

"Congratulations, Brooke."

Needless to say, I left work on cloud nine that day. I had the blessing of and well wishes from my soon-to-be former boss and I was prepared to start the next phase of my career. It felt AMAZING! I knew when I officially made my move that it was going to be bittersweet because I was leaving the familiar and entering the unknown – daring to go and do what no one else before me had done in the history of the firm. But I was cool with that. From where I was standing, there was nowhere I could go but up. Things were finally starting to get better.

Chapter 24

Freedom & Fraud

"Glad to see you back, Brooke," Anita said warmly as she took her seat on the couch across from me. "You look well."

"Always good to see you, Anita," I replied with a smile. "Thank you. You do, too."

"Did you want some water, tea, or coffee?"

"No, thank you."

"Alright, then. So, tell me…what do you hope to accomplish during our session today?"

I took a deep breath and let it out slowly. It had been a minute since I'd seen, much less spoken to Anita and there was a lot I wanted to say. "To sum it up, I came in today to update you on a couple things that happened over the past few months that I'm sure you'll be interested to hear."

Anita sat up just a little straighter, indicating she was intrigued. "I'm all ears. Whenever you're ready."

Four months prior, my divorce from Bishop had been finalized and I was finally a free woman. I had removed my mask and ceased playing the role of The Good Wife. He had put up quite a fight in court, but I walked away with the house and a pretty penny. I started working on redecorating right away because this was no longer just a house, but my home and I wanted it to reflect that fact.

That wasn't the only good thing that happened, though. Not long after that, I had left L. C. Westbrook & Associates and opened my own firm with a dynamic second-to-none team. We had attracted a colorful plethora of clientele – everyone from A-listers to up and coming artists and writers. Business was good. We were getting more established and making a name for ourselves day-by-day and case-by-case. I knew it was still early, but I was convinced that this was the best decision I had made by far.

About a month after the firm had opened, I decided to pay my folks a long overdue visit. Our reunion was sweet to say the least. There was an abundance of hugs and kisses.

Although I was sad to see that Daddy's condition hadn't improved, I was happier to see that it hadn't worsened.

"So, what brings you back home after all this time, baby girl?" Daddy asked as I took a seat on the steps outside. "Was the hustle and bustle of the city getting to be too much for you?"

"...Yes and no. I just wanted to come see you because I was thinking about you not too long ago, and realized how long it had been since I last called, much less saw you, and thought I'd surprise you and Mommy with a visit."

"Well, thank you for making the trip," Mommy said as she came outside, carrying a tray with a pitcher of her delicious orange lemonade and three tall glasses. I jumped up and took the tray from her, set it down on the table next to Daddy, and served the drinks before I returned to my seat on the step. "How long will you be home?" she asked taking her seat next to Daddy.

"Hm...I had planned for a week, if that's all right with you."

Daddy gave Mommy a look that said, 'She's kidding, right?' I had started to think I was imposing until I saw Mommy playfully slap him on the arm, "It's perfectly fine with us, Love!"

We all shared a laugh then sat in silence for a moment before Daddy said, "So, I couldn't help but notice that you made this trip alone. Is there a reason why Ryan isn't with you?"

It was then that I remembered that I hadn't told them, much less anyone back at home about the divorce. I hadn't done that on purpose. It just happened. "Well, Daddy..." I sighed. "Ryan and I are no longer married."

Mommy gasped as she clutched her pearls.

"I meant to tell you both sooner, but I never got around to it."

"Whatever happened?" Mommy asked.

"Let's just say I finally saw what you both tried to tell me about back when I brought him here for the first time. I wish I had listened back then – It would've saved me a lot of time and spared me a lot of trouble. But I finally saw the light and left him."

Daddy didn't say a word, but the look in his eyes was a beautiful combination of joy, pride, and relief knowing that his daughter was free from the very thing he had tried so hard to save her from years before.

Mommy pulled me into a tight embrace. It was almost like she didn't want to let go, but when she did, I looked and saw that she was crying. Not because she was sad, but because she was happy for me and for the new leaf I had turned.

For that entire week, we did nothing but celebrate life, love, and all that God had blessed us with – each other, all that we'd achieved in our lives thus far, and all that would occur in the months and years to come.

I took two more personal days once I got back home to give myself time to readjust and to enjoy the highlights of my trip. On my first day back, I got a call from Cathy saying she wanted to meet with me. I asked what she needed to see me for, and she said that she would much rather tell me in person. I really didn't want to be bothered, but I told her that I would meet her at the café we met at before, the next day.

We met the following day as planned and boy, did she have some tea for me. In addition to Bishop being charged with failure to pay child support by Cathy, and assault by Kelly; he was facing multiple charges of embezzlement and extortion.

After I picked my jaw up off the floor, I asked how she was able to find all this out when I was the one who had the chief investigator. She simply said she had connections and she was almost constantly in the loop because the child support charges involved her children. It made sense, considering I only needed Dexter for the life of my divorce case. But I was blown away by this news. I couldn't help but wonder who Bishop, the man I used to know and love as Ryan, really was. As a matter of fact, I didn't really want to know, considering all the charges stacked up against him.

I was not okay after that meeting with Cathy. I found myself dwelling on Bishop and all the things I didn't know about him. I knew he was a liar based on all the inconsistencies in his stories back when I first found out about him and Cathy, but I didn't know his lies went that far. What was I thinking back when I decided to marry this joker? I really had no idea who I was marrying, much less what I was getting into, but I was glad I came out alive – Bumped, scratched, and a little bruised, but still alive. Then I began to think about all those people – All those lives destroyed because of one man, his pride, his hunger for power, and his impeccable skill in the art of deception.

Bishop didn't have an honest bone in his body. His entire existence was composed of lies and delusions. He lied so much you would think he was the devil, himself. When it came to Bishop, in the words of Billy Joel, honesty was nothing but a lonely word and something hardly ever heard. He could charm or explain his way out of almost any situation and into the heart of anyone who was willing to listen. At least anyone but Mommy, Daddy, and Mother Evans. They saw right through him since day one. It turns out Mother Evans' dream was on point. That man really was dangerously demonic. So much so that he destroyed everything he touched.

I found myself starting to feel guilty for not being vigilant or diligent in getting to know this man before I married him and for letting – no helping – him play me and everyone else for so many years after we got married. But once again I had to remind myself that I was no longer The Good Wife, no longer responsible for covering him, and no longer attached to him or his messes. He was on his own and his theme song could be Baretta's – "don't do the crime if you can't do the time."

It took a while, but I was eventually able to let go and start setting healthy boundaries. I'm still learning and healing from the whole experience.

When I was finished, I looked at Anita and she was trying her best to keep her composure and maintain her professionalism, but she was obviously blown away by everything I had told her.

"W-Wow," she stammered after she managed to pick up her jaw. "Th – That's a lot, even for me…But how – Do you – I'm sorry, I have to figure out what I'm trying to ask."

"It's fine," I assured her as she took her time to formulate a question in response to this mass of new information.

"I'll keep it simple. Are you okay?"

"Yes."

"Are you sure? Are you well physically, mentally, emotionally, and even spiritually?"

"Again, yes."

"Okay," she sighed in what seemed to be relief. "…Would you consider yourself to be in a better place now than you were when we last met?"

"I'd say so," I said with a smile. "But like I said, I'm still learning and healing. Taking one day at a time. Some days are better than others."

Anita looked like she was still trying to process everything I told her, determine whether to ask another question, or think about what she should say next. "Well, that's wonderful, Brooke. I sure missed a lot, haven't I? But, I'm glad to see that you've moved on and you aren't allowing yourself to be drawn back into your ex-husband's nonsense. He made his bed, now he has to lie in it."

"Thank you, Anita. You know I wouldn't have made it this far without you, either."

"You know I got you, girl. My line and my door are always open. So, tell me…with your divorce and life as first lady behind you and a brand-new career path before you, what's next?"

"Well…" Though I had many plans and aspirations, I was thinking the main thing is to trust the process – continue advancing in my field, working on me, enjoying life, and prayerfully eventually find real love. I answered Anita, "Time will tell."

Chapter 25

Beginning Again

I had just left Anita's and hopped into my car with the intention to grab some lunch when my phone started ringing. Someone wanted to FaceTime me. I sighed because all I wanted was to turn on my jams, be on my way, and get some food. Normally, I'd ignore it because I was rarely in the mood for it, but I decided to check just to see who was trying to reach me. *Well, then,* I thought upon seeing the image of my own personal sexy, silver-eyed Adonis plastered on the screen. *I suppose I'll make an exception.* "Hey, Baby!"

"Hello, Beautiful," David said, flashing the biggest smile. "How are you? It's been a while."

"Well, who's fault is that?" I asked playfully.

"Play fair, Baby. We're both two adults living in the fast lane, which makes it hard for us to connect on a regular basis. You know we're always missing each other. I'm just glad I was able to catch you today!"

"Me, too." We normally communicated via text message, so this FaceTime session was a welcome change in routine. "Are you on your lunch break?"

"My lunch is actually over in three minutes," he admitted, "but I just wanted to try my luck and see if I could get in touch with you and your gorgeous self. When can I see you?"

"You're looking right at me, Babe."

David sucked his teeth. "You know what I mean. Stop playing. This digital thing isn't working for me anymore, Brooke. I want to be in the same space as you, breathe the same air, see the same sights, and just be in your presence."

"Me too, Love." He was right. It had been far too long since we had last been together. *Wow...Was the conference that long ago? Dang.*

"So, how are we going to do this?" he asked. "I could come see you, you could come see me, or we could even meet halfway. I wouldn't mind getting away – having a little rendezvous someplace tropical with bright blue water and white sandy beaches, what do you think?"

"...Surprise me."

"Okay."

He tried his hardest to stay past his three minutes, but I made sure he went back to work. I even got to see his office because of it. But once he hung up, I had to fight to resist the urge to call him back. Had it really been that long since we last spoke, much less saw each other? Was this love? *Distance **does** make the heart fonder…I'll settle for maybe.* With that, I drove off to get my fix of a loaded chicken enchilada with a side of maduros.

2 Weeks Later

It was Saturday and instead of sleeping in, I thought it would be a good idea to do some cleaning around the house. After devising my plan of attack, I turned up my oldies and got to cleaning. I dusted, swept, polished, and mopped all within two hours. I was about get the vacuum when I got a phone call from a certain Adonis. "Hello?"

"Hello, mi amor," David seemed to purr. "Where are you?"

"…I'm at home. Why?"

"No reason. Just wondering where you were. 'Kay, bye."

I squinted at my phone like, *What?* That whole conversation was strange because David had never called just to ask where I was. I mulled over it for a minute but couldn't make sense of it, so I went ahead and got the vacuum to finish my cleaning day.

About an hour and a half later, I was relaxing on the couch in the living room when David called again. *What in the world is going on?* I thought.

"Hey, Baby, it's me again," he said warmly.

"Is everything okay?"

"Everything's fine. Why do you ask?"

"Because you've never called me twice in one day."

"Uh…I actually have, Love. I have the receipts to prove it, too."

*Oh, he **does**?* "Alright, then. We'll confirm that later, but what's up?" I could sense that he was up to something, but I couldn't tell what.

"…You still home?" he asked hesitantly.

"Yeah. Why does it matter whether I'm home?"

"Well-," The doorbell rang. "Were you expecting company?"

"N-No, but-," The doorbell rang again.

"Sounds urgent…"

"They can wait."

"Are you sure?" he asked. The doorbell rang two times in a row.

"Just a minute!" I yelled. "Now, why does it matter-," Three times in a row. Then came knocking. *You know what?* "I'm sorry, Babe. Let me go see who this is."

"Okay," he said coolly.

"I'm coming!" I yelled as I made my way to the door. I saw a tall silhouette through the frosted glass and hesitated. Whoever it was knocked again and shifted their weight from one foot to the other as they waited. Did they know I was here?

Before they could knock again, I snatched the door open. I was about to demand who they were and what they wanted but stopped upon seeing David standing there with his hands in his pockets and a smug look on his face. I dropped my phone and was in his arms in an instant, my face buried in his chest as I took in the scent of his cologne – that intoxicating combination of leather, black pepper, and tobacco I loved so much.

He let me have my moment before he pulled away and tilted my head up so I could look at him. "I got you good, didn't I?" he teased.

"I should've known!" I pouted as I jabbed him in the arm.

"Well, you *did* say to surprise you, so…" he said with a shrug.

"But *you* said something about a rendezvous…Was that to throw me off?"

"Maybe, maybe not. No, I'm kidding. It was to throw you off, but what I said was true. I wouldn't mind taking a little island getaway with you, but only if you want to, of course."

That's what I loved about David. He was honest and sweet; never forceful. He always made a point to respect and be mindful of my boundaries and preferences. "I'd like that, too. But let's get you inside and off the street!"

Once we got in the house and got comfortable in the living room, David told me all about his flight, the drive into the city, where and how long he planned to stay, and how he came up with the whole plan. It never ceased to amaze me how much attention to detail he paid. He admitted that the phone call was improvised on his part because it could have gone completely sideways, but it worked out regardless. It turns out that he was planning to stay for a week. He said he could stay longer if that's what I wanted, but I told him that a week was fine for now. That was most likely to change, but I didn't want to be too greedy; not that he would mind.

We decided that we would spend the day in Greenwich and save our island getaway for some other time. I began his introduction to my former home town with some sightseeing since it was his first time there. I threw in a few of my personal favorite spots so David wouldn't get too bored with the usual tourist traps. We ended the day with dinner and a movie that David paid for. Like last time, he wouldn't let me leave the tip. For the movie, he ordered everything large. When we got back to my house in Stamford, he walked me to the door, bid me good night, and kissed me on the forehead. He would have walked away, but I grabbed him by the collar and pulled him back and kissed him so fiercely it made up for all the ones I missed in all the months we spent apart. Needless to say, he staggered the whole way back to his car.

The days that followed were like a movie. They were filled with lunch dates, walks in the park, late night drives, window shopping, talking all night until the sun came up, and even guitar serenades – the kind of things you'd hear about in any classic 90s Black Love story. Again, I found myself falling fast and hard for this man who had proven what I meant to him not just by what he did by coming all this way to visit, but in the way he treated me. When I spoke, he listened intently – not just to what I was saying, but to what I wasn't saying. He remembered the little things about me that most people would miss or forget. And he was a gentleman in every sense of the word. The chemistry between us was undeniable. Anyone could look at us and tell that there was a force greater than love that drew us together.

One day, we were at the mall and just so happened to wander into a jewelry store. I didn't realize what was going on until it had happened. David tried to play it off like we were just browsing when in fact, he was trying to figure out my ring size and what type of rings I liked.

I took it in stride, but on the drive back to my place, I had to break it to him that I loved him, I could see a future with him, and I wanted it more than anything in the world, but I had to take my time getting there. I had rushed in the past and look where it got me. I wasn't afraid. I wasn't unsure. I just wanted our forever to be a long, slow one. David understood and didn't push the issue. He continued to shower me with love and affection until he left for New York the following week.

After I watched his plane take off, I left the airport, got in my car, and turned on my Spotify. Fate would have it that the illustrious Phyllis Hyman would grace my ears with the exact approach I said I wanted to take in this relationship with David. *Follow the book that's my intention, The book of life, The book of love.* Yeah, that was plan – Take things slow, continue to heal and grow, and see where this road would lead.

SETTING THE CAPTIVES
FREE
MINISTRIES

DR. CAROL LYNN PATTERSON

www.setcaptivesfree.com

National Domestic Violence Hotline
1-800-799-7233
OR
Text START to 88788

Scan the QR code to hear the *Deceit* playlist

Follow the author on social media

Made in the USA
Middletown, DE
18 August 2022